The
CURSED
FRIEND

The
CURSED
FRIEND

A Novel

BEATRICE SALVIONI

Translated from the Italian by Elena Pala

HarperVia

An Imprint of HarperCollins*Publishers*

THE CURSED FRIEND. Copyright © 2023 by Beatrice Salvioni. All rights reserved. Printed in the United States of America. No part of this book may be used or reproduced in any manner whatsoever without written permission except in the case of brief quotations embodied in critical articles and reviews. For information, address HarperCollins Publishers, 195 Broadway, New York, NY 10007.

English translation copyright © 2024 by Elena Pala.

HarperCollins books may be purchased for educational, business, or sales promotional use. For information, please email the Special Markets Department at SPsales@harpercollins.com.

Originally published as *La Malnata* in Italy in 2023 by Giulio Einaudi Editore.

First HarperVia hardcover published 2024

FIRST EDITION

Designed by Yvonne Chan

Library of Congress Cataloging-in-Publication Data has been applied for.

ISBN 978-0-06-323400-0

24 25 26 27 28 LBC 5 4 3 2 1

To the girl I once was.

And above all, to those who taught me

never to stop listening to her.

CONTENTS

Prologue
Don't Tell a Soul 1

Part I
Where the World Begins and Ends 5

Part II
Today's Sins, Tomorrow's Blood 91

Part III
The Test of True Courage 127

Part IV
The Severed Tongue of a Goose 165

Epilogue
The Shape of a Voice 209

Acknowledgments   219
A Note from the Translator   223

The
CURSED
FRIEND

PROLOGUE

Don't Tell a Soul

I t's hard to get a dead body off yours.

I found out at the age of twelve, blood streaming down my nose and mouth, panties twisted around my ankles. My back was deep in mud on the banks of the Lambro, shingle sharp as fingernails biting into my neck and bare buttocks. His body was heavy on my belly, all hard edges, still warm. A glazed, blank look had settled on his face and white froth was gathering on his chin, a foul smell emanating from his parted lips. He'd looked at me before he collapsed, fear twisting his features, a hand still fumbling in his pants. His dilated, inky pupils seemed to pool and spill over his cheeks, then he'd slumped onto me, his knees still pinning my thighs open. He wasn't moving anymore.

"I just wanted him to stop," said Maddalena, pawing at a clump of mud, blood, and tangled hair on her head. "I had to do it, I had no choice."

She started walking toward me, the light dress she wore clinging to her wet skin and outlining a stark, sinewy figure. "I'm coming!" she said. "Don't move."

But I hadn't managed to move at all: my body was like an

abandoned, alien shell, a tooth that had fallen out of its mouth. All I felt was blood on my tongue and lips as I struggled to breathe. Maddalena dropped to her hands and knees next to me, shingle crunching under her naked legs. Her socks were soaked and she was missing a shoe. She began pushing at his chest with both arms, using her elbows, then her forehead. She kept trying, but the body wouldn't budge.

Things are heavier when they're dead, like that cat in Noè's backyard, covered in dirt, sticky guts peeking out of his stomach and a cloud of flies feasting on his snout and eyes. We'd buried him together, behind the goose pen.

"I won't manage by myself," said Maddalena, wet hair sticking to her forehead and dripping on the pebbles. "You have to help."

Her voice sloshed around my skull, louder and louder. With great effort, I managed to slide one arm from under his body, then the other. I pressed my palms against his chest and pushed. Above us, the arches of the bridge and a square of murky sky. Below, slippery wet pebbles. All around us, the roar of the river.

"You have to give it one big push."

I did as I was told. With every breath I inhaled the sweet, sickening scent of his cologne.

Maddalena looked at me. "Now!" she ordered.

We pushed together. I let out a piercing cry, arched my spine, and suddenly he peeled off, flopping on his back next to me, eyes and mouth wide open, pants pooling at his knees, belt buckle clattering on the stones.

As soon as I felt the weight lift from my body, I turned on one side, spitting red saliva on the pebbles, rubbing my fingers over my nostrils and lips to wipe off his smell. For a moment I felt like the air was being sucked out of my lungs, then I curled my legs against my belly and tried to breathe again. The elastic band on my panties had snapped and the fabric was torn where it had gathered under my heel. I angrily kicked them off and pulled down my skirt, which was bunched up above my navel. My belly was cold and I ached all over.

Maddalena stood, wiping her palms on her thighs to scrub off the mud. "Are you all right?" she asked. I bit my lip and nodded. My throat felt like a dam about to crack, but I didn't cry—Maddalena had taught me well. Crying was for idiots. Her eyes small and hard, she raked the wet hair off her forehead then pointed at the body: "We've no hope of moving him too far. We'll have to hide him here," she continued, licking the dried blood under her nose.

I rose to my feet and joined her. My legs were quaking, the smooth soles of my shoes kept slipping on the wet stones, and I held on to her, fingers wrapped around her wrist. The smell of the river blocked everything out, and Maddalena was shaking, but it wasn't fear. She wasn't afraid of anything, not of the dog with swollen gums and white froth on his teeth, not of Tresoldi, not of the devil's leg down the chimney in that scary story the grown-ups loved to tell. Not even of blood, not even of war. She was shaking because she was drenched. He'd grabbed her by the hair and dragged her into the Lambro kicking and screaming, then plunged her head underwater to silence her, all the while crooning a popular song, *"Parlami d'amore Mariù,"* his voice raspy like the ones we'd hear on the radio.

"We need to find some branches," Maddalena said, "sturdy branches." But she kept staring at that motionless frame, all dips and rises, who only minutes before had been clasping my wrists as his tongue thrust inside my mouth. I could still feel it, that tongue, his fingers, his breath on me. All I wanted was to sleep—right there, on the shingle, surrounded by the roar of the river. But Maddalena laid a hand on my shoulder and said: "We better hurry."

We rolled the body away from the shore and dragged it up to one of the pillars of the bridge, then dropped it in a heap against the moist, oozing bricks, elbows jutting out at an unnatural angle, fingers like claws, mouth wide open. There was no trace of the elegant, arrogant young man he'd been, pressed pants and Fascist Party pin glinting on his lapel—the man who'd smooth his hair with a tortoiseshell comb and laugh as he told us, "You're nothing." We gathered some branches that had got tangled between the duck nests and the drainage canals during the last flood and placed them on the body, now half-sunk in the water. Then we piled roots and rocks on top of it so it wouldn't be carried off by the next flood.

"We have to close his eyes," Maddalena said as she dropped the last rock, big as a fist. "That's what you're supposed to do with the dead. I've seen it done."

"I don't want to touch him."

"All right. I'll do it." She laid the palm of her hand on that ashen face, lowering his lids with her thumb and middle finger. Lying there with his eyes closed and his mouth wide open, tucked under a blanket of branches and rocks, he looked like someone who'd been caught in a nightmare, unable to wake up. We wrung our skirts and socks, then Maddalena removed the one shoe she still had and stashed it in her pocket. I did the same with my panties, now a sodden, muddy rag I plucked from the pebbles.

"I have to go now," she said.

"When will I see you?"

"Soon."

As I walked home, socks squeaking inside my shoes, I thought of the time before it all began. Less than a year ago, my skirt had been dry and uncreased as I pressed my belly against the parapet on Leoni bridge to watch Maddalena, far below. The only thing I knew about her was that she brought bad luck. I was yet to learn that a word from her was all it took to save you or doom you, the only difference between walking home in drenched socks and sleeping forever, face down in the river.

Part I

Where

the

WORLD

BEGINS

and

ENDS

1.

*T*hey called her the Cursed One and nobody liked her.

Saying her name brought bad luck. She was a witch, one of those who can mark you with the scent of death. She had the devil inside, and I was never to talk to her. I would watch her from a distance on Sundays, when Mom made me wear the shoes that sliced my heels, clumpy stockings, and my best dress, which I had to take care not to soil. Sweat would drip down my neck and the constant chafing reddened my thighs.

That Sunday, the Cursed One was down on the banks of the Lambro with the boys, two kids I knew by name only: Filippo Colombo, arms and legs like chicken bones, and Matteo Fossati, shoulders and chest the size of a side of beef, like those you'd see glinting with fat at the San Francesco market. Both sported shorts and scraped knees, and for her—who was younger, and a girl to boot—they'd have gladly taken a bullet, like soldiers in the war, and then met their maker with a resigned "I can die happy."

The hem of her skirt, faded by the sun and dirt, was tucked into the belt that cinched her waist—a man's belt—her bare feet firmly planted on the sun-warmed rocks. That's the one thing a girl ought never to show: her legs. Maddalena's were bare and streaked with mud, scabbed like a stray dog whose wounds are never seen to. She was laughing, a thrashing fish trying to escape her grip. The boys were clapping and stomping their feet, sending dark river water splashing all around as I spied on them from the bridge. I was on my way to the 11 a.m. service, which my mother maintained was the one attended by "good society."

"We're going to be late!" she huffed, tugging at my arm and glancing over the parapet. "Ragamuffins!"

My father was a few steps ahead of us, walking briskly with his hands clasped behind his back, the nape of his neck barely visible under his hat. He said nothing. He could not bear to scold, but I knew all too well, and my mother even better, that were we to fall more than a stone's throw behind him and make us all late for church, that would be a day of strained silences, of slammed doors and teeth gritting on the bit of his pipe behind the Sunday papers. I had to make a conscious effort to peel my gaze away from the kids by the river, the kids I'd always spied on, the kids I'd never be. But that Sunday, for the first time, the Cursed One looked straight at me with her gleaming black eyes. Then she smiled.

My breath caught. I shut my eyes and darted up the street that led to the cathedral to join my father. I fell into step beside him but he hadn't noted my absence. The few cars driving by forced us to flatten against the shop windows—the haberdasher's, the baker's with a sign advertising trays of pastries for five lira, a warm scent of vanilla wafting out the door. Roberto Colombo's black Fiat Balilla inched past us. He worked for the city council and "knew people in high places," as my father often remarked in a grave tone. Colombo wore black knee-high boots and had two sons, who Mrs. Colombo insisted wear their hair with a center parting. When the old ladies at the church informed him that his youngest spent his days down at the Lambro with the Cursed One, rumor had it he'd forced a whole bottle of castor oil down his throat and tanned his hide. For a while, it had been just Matteo and the Cursed One by the river on Sundays: Filippo sat in church on the same bench as his father, just a foot away, shirt buttoned all the way up and shiny loafers. I was secretly glad to see him there. Then, one day, Filippo had gone back to splashing in the mud, and his family had taken to sitting farther apart on their bench, hoping people wouldn't notice the empty spot.

Colombo's car was always perfectly polished, the grid on the nose resembling the sharp teeth of a shark. He always parked it on the square right outside the church, as if he was afraid to ruin his boots by taking a few steps. My father's lips twitched as they did when flecks of tobacco got stuck in his teeth. "The death of us," he muttered. "Those infernal machines will be the death of us." There was nothing he detested more than cars. "All people care about is going fast," he'd say. "That's why no one wants to wear hats anymore." If he came across Mr. Colombo, however, he'd greet him politely, tipping his gray felt fedora.

As we entered the church, the unbearable heat that had descended on the town two weeks before the official start of summer subsided. There was only the musty stench of incense that shot straight up to your brain and spread down to your toes, like fear of the dark. My hand clasped in my mother's, I took care to only step on the white marble tiles: the bronze-and-gold Jesus over the altar wouldn't stop looking at me, and if I happened to step on one of the black ones, I'd be going straight to hell. Muttered litanies and the sound of smacking lips filled the central nave as the old women prayed, hunched over the pews, heads hidden under veils that covered their ears. We would always occupy one of the benches near the front, and I had to keep perfectly quiet, except to repeat the appropriate verses during the psalms, and saying "Amen" and *"Mea culpa, mea maxima culpa."* As the priest rattled on about sins and hell, I thought about silver-bellied fish, kids playing barefoot in the river, and the Cursed One's eyes.

2.

*F*ace hidden in her hands, my mother recited the Our Father, the pads of her fingers grazing her eyelids. I studied a nail that stuck out of the wood on the kneeling stool. When the priest raised his arms over his head holding the holy wafer, I dropped on my knees like the old women did. I felt around for the nail then bore down on it with all my weight. I interlaced my fingers and pressed them against my mouth, pushing the knuckles through my teeth while I scraped my knee hard over the nail and sang the Glory hymn. I rubbed and rubbed until pain shot through my skull, scorching hot and smooth. I wanted scars on my knees like the kids down at the Lambro. I wanted to feel the river flow through my toes and bare my muddy legs. I wanted the boys to clap their hands and stomp their feet in the water for me.

The Cursed One always strolled through town shuffling her worn sandals on the cobblestones, chin jutting forward, flanked by two older boys. When they saw her, the women would cross themselves, hissing a "Lord have mercy" through gritted teeth; the men would spit on the ground. She'd laugh out loud and stick her tongue out, bobbing a mock curtsy, as if to thank them for the insult. Her uneven jet-black hair looked like it had been chopped with a blunt knife, and her dark eyes glinted like those of a cat. Her legs were the legs of a cat too, wiry and nimble, and I thought she was the most beautiful creature I had ever seen.

The first time she talked to me was four days after that Sunday when her gaze had plunged into mine from across the bridge parapet. It was June 6, 1935, the Feast of Saint Gerard. The square outside the cathedral was teeming with people, busier than on Easter Sunday, porticoes and balconies festooned with bunting and flower garlands. Every year, the procession made its way into the church to pay homage to the remains of the saint: worshippers crossed themselves and kissed the tips of their fingers before laying them gently on the glass shrine housing a skeleton in a golden robe, then came out for air into the light of the square.

The church bells tolled plaintively under heat-laden clouds. Street vendors hawking candy and tin toys crowded the porticoes and the mulberry grove in the cloister, right next to the shooting gallery. Tresoldi, the greengrocer, stood behind his stall, arms crossed over his chest and a vicious look on his face, waiting for customers. He smelled of musty towels. "Cherries!" he bellowed, gripping the counter with his beefy hands. "Three lira for a bag of cherries!" His son, Noè, whose face bore the marks of his father's temper, piled up crates against the columns. Shirtsleeves rolled up above his elbows like a grown man, Noè was only three years older than me, but he'd been taken out of school early. People said the greengrocer had always hated his son, and the proof was in the name he'd chosen for him. Noè had come with the flood one November. The river had burst its banks, destroying bridges and flooding basements, and he'd burst out of his mother, draining all the blood out of her. He'd only thought to save himself, like Noah, who loaded the animals on his ark without sparing a thought for his fellow human beings, abandoned by the Lord under the deluge.

The heat that day was the kind of overbearing midday swelter that, on festive occasions, would see the town's women neatly divided into two categories, each taking great pains never to mix with the other: there were those who could afford white gloves and light polka-dot dresses just below the knee, and those who only ever wore the same thick dress to all weddings and first communions, regardless of the season. Then there were the maids in their uniforms, but they kept to the opposite side of the street, spying the stalls from a distance as they briskly walked by, shopping list clasped in their fist and a bag laden with supplies in the crook of their elbow.

I walked hand in hand with my mother, who wore a pink straw fascinator with a ribbon that kept bouncing on her cheek. She'd bought a cluster of papier-mâché cherries at the haberdasher's and secured it to the hat with a length of wire. Mom was desperate for other women to envy her, especially those who walked around bareheaded and could only look at the stalls, because the cherries were too expensive. But she was not content with putting on airs with factory workers' wives—she smiled at their husbands too.

My father, suit jacket hanging loose from his shoulders, stood by the shooting gallery. He had removed his hat and was tormenting the brim with his fingernails. Next to him, Colombo was pointing a tin rifle at the metal figurines as passersby jerked their arm up in greeting, fingers jutting forward. Colombo appeared intent on firing cork pellets at those figurines as if they were enemies in a real war. The front of his black shirt was heavy with medals, and every now and again his thumb grazed the pin with the Italian tricolor and the symbol of the National Fascist Party, as if to straighten it.

Not far, opposite the baker's stall that smelled of honey and fritters, Mr. Fossati stood with his thumbs hooked in his belt loops, yellow blotches staining his worn vest beneath the arms. He was laughing and pointing at the shooting gallery, surrounded by men whose cheeks were already ruddy with wine. Fossati was fond of saying that Colombo's medals had been raided from coffins, that he boasted of earning them in God knows what battle, when they were no more than amateur tournament trophies or family heirlooms. He also said that Colombo was just a boy who liked to play war, but he'd never even seen a real rifle. Colombo, for his part, said that the only thing Fossati ever did to support peace was drinking to it at the Saint Gerard Inn, only to then throw it up, together with all that Lambrusco, behind the water mills. Everyone knew about these things, even us children, because what happened in other families was the favorite topic of conversation on Sundays, when friends would come over for lunch and we had to remain seated at the table until the end of the meal and "mind our manners."

"Will you get me some cherries?" I pleaded, tugging at my mother's arm and pointing at Tresoldi's stall.

"You know very well what your father said."

Your father. When something bothered or displeased her, it invariably became someone else's fault. "Your father says we are not going on holiday this year" or "Your father says we should only keep the one maid." I, too, became "your daughter" when I had to be disciplined—an unwanted present, discarded and soon forgotten at the bottom of a wardrobe.

"Can I at least look?"

"At the cherries, you mean? All right." My mother let go of my hand.

"But do behave. Don't touch anything."

She straightened the elaborate coiffure kept together by dozens of hairpins under her hat and made for the shooting gallery. When she joined my father, Colombo lifted the toy rifle: "Would you like me to win something for you, Mrs. Strada?" he teased. I balled my hands into fists, toes curling inside my tight shoes. Mom giggled, covering her mouth with her hand. Colombo casually grazed her hip, then his fingers stole up to her elbow, stroking it. Suddenly he turned and looked at me, a frown on his brow like Mussolini's in the portrait that hangs in our classroom. He smiled. I felt his eyes on me and stiffened all over, then I ran, shame lodged in my throat, and stopped a few yards from Tresoldi's stall.

I was fascinated by the little paper bags full of gleaming dark cherries, but I kept my distance, intimidated by him. I stood in the shade of the cathedral, fingers interlaced behind my back, my mother's words floating through my mind: don't touch anything.

"What are you doing? Looking at the cherries?" someone croaked behind me, shaking me from my reverie.

Behind me stood the Cursed One. She was leaning against the wall with the faded fresco of Saint Gerard, the pockets of her torn dress heavy with pebbles, looking me up and down. My breath caught, and all of a sudden the ground seemed to slip from under my feet. We'd never been that close. She smelled like river water, and a pale scar ran from under her nose to the bow of her upper lip. A ruddy, sheeny mark covered part of her cheek from her temple down to her chin.

"Wh-what?" To my dismay, I realized I was stuttering like I did as a little girl when I had to recite the alphabet, the nuns ready to correct my mistakes with the flick of a ruler on my fingers.

"The cherries," she reprised. "Don't you want them?"

"I can't. I don't have any money."

"Don't you now?" she bit back, eyeing me with an air of superiority although she was a good three inches shorter than me. "These are rich people clothes. You've even got shiny shoes!" she sniggered, pointing at my feet. Her laughter was loud and coarse and she made no attempt to disguise it.

"So what?" I retorted, trying to hold my chin up.

"So you do have the money for the cherries."

"Me? No," I said. "My father does. But he doesn't want me to have the cherries."

"Why not?"

I looked down at my shoe. "Because."

"But why?"

"And what do you care?"

"Take them, then," she blurted out.

"How? I told you I haven't any money."

"Just take them."

We had a crucifix at home, a large, dark one that didn't smell of wood anymore, only wax. Mom and Dad kept it in their bedroom, hanging over their bed, together with the silver holy water stoups and the framed photos of their wedding. When they left the door open, Jesus's wooden eyes could see all the way into my room, and I couldn't sleep.

"Jesus is always watching you," my mother was fond of saying, after listing all the things good girls ought and ought not to do. Whenever a "bad thought" (as my mother called them) crossed my mind—such as stealing a chocolate from the bowl and then hiding the golden wrapper in the vase on my bedside table, or fussing at bedtime, or touching myself between my legs until I shook all over before falling asleep—I imagined Jesus's sad wooden eyes on me, and I froze, paralyzed, fear and guilt coursing all the way down to my toes. I felt dirty and wrong because wooden Jesus could peer into my head and see all my sins, even the most secret ones.

The day the Cursed One spoke to me for the first time and told me to take the cherries, I answered: "It's not done." The world was a place of rules that couldn't be broken, a place of grown-up things, large and dangerous, of irreparable mistakes that would kill you or send you to jail. A terrifying place fraught with forbidden activities, where you had to tiptoe around making sure not to touch anything. Especially if you were a girl.

That bag of bones set her jaw and said: "Watch. Watch me now."

And I, a sense of urgency knotting my stomach, did as I was told. Watching her was something I'd always done—but this was different, now she was asking me to.

The Cursed One turned her back on me and stepped out of the shaded area by the church. Her jet-black hair gleaming in the sun, she raised a hand as you do in class when you know the answer to a question. As soon as she lowered it, Filippo Colombo's straight blond hair and Matteo Fossati's bulky, dark frame emerged from behind a column, Matteo in a stained vest identical to his father's: the two boys who stomped their feet in the river for the Cursed One. They approached Tresoldi's stall, circling it as they whispered to each other, drawing attention to themselves.

The greengrocer was scolding his son, Noè: "Dimwit!" he shouted angrily, "You still asleep or what?"

Noè passively submitted to his tirade as he kept piling crates.

Filippo and Matteo paused by the cherry stall. Tresoldi stopped swearing and shot them an ominous look, his bloodshot eyes glinting like cherry stones with bits of red pulp attached to them. In a deliberately slow movement, Matteo reached for a bag of cherries, picked one up by the stem, and lifted it to his lips. Filippo hesitated. Matteo jabbed an elbow into his side and he doubled over like a snapped stick, then grabbed a cherry and quickly shoved it into his mouth, shaking with fear.

"You louts!" Tresoldi yelled. He reached under the counter to pull out a long stick with a small hook at one end, the kind used to lower shutters, and bashed it against one of the columns. The noise startled Noè, and the crates he'd been piling tumbled to the ground. Matteo and Filippo darted down the porticoes through skirts and flower garlands, laughing, while Tresoldi slid out from behind the counter and chased after them, consumed by a dark rage. He limped, leaning on his stick or wielding it ominously when he stopped, propping himself up on one of the columns to catch his breath. The previous winter they'd had to amputate all the toes on one of his feet after he'd fallen asleep in the snow, clutching a bottle.

Nothing terrified me more than Tresoldi's rotting, severed black toes. People said he'd fed them to the geese in his backyard, who had since acquired a taste for human flesh. While Tresoldi hobbled through the crowd and Noè picked up the scattered crates, the Cursed One sauntered to the stall, picked up a bag of cherries, and calmly walked away from the porticoes heading toward the main street, an angelic smile pasted on her face.

I watched her disappear into the crowd and noticed, somewhat resentfully, that I was still alive. My skull hadn't been crushed by a fallen roof tile, my lungs hadn't squeezed the breath out of me, my heart hadn't suddenly stopped beating. I had spoken to the Cursed One, looked her in the eye, and the devil hadn't come to wrench my soul out of my ears. When the greengrocer came back, sweat dripping from his forehead, he noticed the empty spot where the stolen bag of cherries had been, and swore out loud. He looked all around him and even up to the sky, as if the angels themselves might have taken it. He stomped his good foot, grabbed Noè by the collar of his filthy shirt, and resumed his swearing, as if to cover the loud slaps he rained on his son.

"Where the hell were you, huh?" he shouted.

Noè lifted his arms to shield his face from his father's blows. "There was another one and you let him get away . . . right under your nose! You dumbhead!"

I mustered some courage and approached the cherry stall: "I saw him." I said. I had to repeat it again before Tresoldi turned to face me, his features crumpled like stale focaccia bread left out in the sun.

"You're the Strada girl," he growled, dropping Noè's shirt and causing him to lose his balance and fall. "So? Where'd he go?"

I pointed to the back of the church, near the cloister, and answered, "That way." That's all I said, because lies made my tongue trip in between syllables. Tresoldi started out toward the cloister, limping, and I watched him until he disappeared behind the apse and the sound of his steps died out.

I was panting, waiting for the inevitable punishment—for the paved square to crack open and swallow me whole, for an enormous, all-powerful, bleeding hand with a nail stuck in it to part the sky and smite me. Nothing happened. Maybe the wooden Jesus was looking the other way and he wasn't paying attention when I lied. Or maybe lying wasn't a sin. And seeing as the ground had also failed to crack open under the Cursed One's feet, then stealing Tresoldi's cherries wasn't a sin either. And if, after talking to her and concealing the truth, I had yet to die, then perhaps it was the grown-ups who had lied to me.

Noè had got up to his feet and was looking at me with a strange spark in his eyes, wiping his face with his sleeve. I started walking backward, slowly at first, as in a game of hide-and-seek. Then, suddenly, I broke into a run and bolted through the porticoes and bunting, the crowd thinning as I approached the street that led to the riverbank.

I saw them from a distance: three silhouetted figures against the blue sky, perched on the parapet of San Gerardino bridge, which sat opposite the square with the white church and led to the taverns. I stepped closer. The Cursed One's legs dangled over the dark river as she pointed at the statue of Saint Gerard, floating in the middle of the river on a small raft secured to the bridge with ropes. Saint Gerard was made of wood, dressed like a monk, and kneeling on the raft blanketed in pine needles, a bag of cherries next to him. It was my father who told me about the miracle he'd performed, how he'd used his cloak as a raft to bring food to the sick during the flood, the year the bridge had collapsed. That is why, on the Feast of Saint Gerard, the statue was lowered onto the river. The cherries represented a different miracle: the saint had made them appear in winter, when snow falls and no fruit can grow.

The stolen bag of cherries sat on the stone parapet: they had already eaten more than half. Flanking the Cursed One like saints either side of the Virgin Mary were the two boys. She chewed like men chew, loudly and with her mouth open. Then she'd tilt her head backward and spit the cherry stone far out and down into the dark waters of the Lambro. She was laughing, pointing at the statue of the saint or the little waterfall farther down, where branches and black mud stuck to the mill wheel. The boys laughed with her, their legs dangling from the parapet, arguing over who could spit the farthest.

"I want one too," I interjected.

They all spun around to face me at once.

"You have to give me at least one."

Matteo and Filippo stared at me as if I was a rotting carcass, then turned to the Cursed One. It was she who said: "What for?"

"Because I helped you."

"No, you didn't."

"Yes, I did."

"We took the cherries. You just stood there and watched," she shot back.

"That's not true!" I replied. "Tresoldi came back, and I lied to him. If I hadn't, he'd have found you."

"So even rich girls in fine clothes can tell lies?"

I crumpled my skirt.

"And what did you tell him?"

"That he'd gone the other way. To the cloister."

"Who?"

"The thief."

"Do you think I'm a thief?" she asked, her black eyes boring a hole through me.

"You took the cherries," I said. What sounded like a simple question was in fact like those math exercises where, once you've solved one equation, you have to solve another and then another, and then you get all mixed up and have to start over.

"You didn't leave him any money," I continued, cautiously, my eyes fixed on her red-stained lips. "That's called stealing."

She rolled a cherry stone inside her mouth and spat it into her fist. "Do you know what used to be where Tresoldi's shop is now?" she asked. I shook my head. Matteo and Filippo kept eating cherries and spitting the stones in the river.

Tresoldi's shop was at the corner of Via Vittorio Emanuele, opposite the tobacconist's. The neighborhood's ladies often headed there after the 4 p.m. service. Tresoldi lived in the apartment behind the shop, and he also had a yard where he kept a scruffy dog with red gums chained to a post, and a pen for his geese and chickens.

The Cursed One rolled a cherry stem between her fingers. "There was a butcher shop. Meat hooks, slicers, the works. But the owner was kicked out to make room for the greengrocer's."

Matteo's face darkened, then he turned and stared at the river.

"But why?" I asked.

"Because if you're not careful, the Fascists won't even let you keep the clothes on your back," answered Matteo.

Hearing those words, Filippo shuddered and began gnawing at his knuckles, as if he somehow felt responsible for what had happened to the butcher. The Cursed One nodded gravely, picked up a handful of cherries, and chewed them quickly, then spat out all the stones at once. They clattered to the ground like hail on cobblestones.

"Can you do that?"

"I don't know."

"Have a go," she challenged me, making room on the parapet next to her.

I laid my hands on the flagstone and tried to hoist myself up, but it was too high and I kept slipping.

Filippo, a cherry stem dangling from the gap between his front teeth, burst out laughing. "She can't do it!" he sneered, but the Cursed One silenced him with a glance and pulled me up, grabbing me beneath the arms, then dropped the bag between her thighs.

"Take one and spit the stone as far as you can."

I obeyed. The cherry was soft against the roof of my mouth and tasted faintly of dirt.

"If you swallow the stone, you might die."

"I won't," I replied, chewing carefully, feeling around for the stone with my teeth. "Did you think I didn't know that?"

"Watch me. That's how it's done."

I observed her carefully as she arched her back and sucked her lips in, preparing to propel the stone far out into the river. I tried to do the same, but while hers, Matteo's, and Filippo's landed in the water near the statue of Saint Gerard—and at times even smacked against the wooden raft—mine slipped limply down the pillars of the bridge.

"I can't do it."

"You just have to practice. It's easy," she reassured me. "Try again."

I chewed the next cherry thoroughly, rolling the stone around, cleaning every last bit of pulp with my tongue until I felt it smooth against the roof of my mouth.

"You!" someone shouted at the other end of the bridge.

Tresoldi's cheeks were blotched purple, his rolled-up sleeves exposing sturdy, hairy forearms. "It was you who stole my cherries, you thugs!"

The Cursed One flinched, but was quick to nudge the bag of cherries into the Lambro as she wiped her lips on the back of her hand.

Tresoldi strode forward; I could already smell his fetid breath. That's when I realized I was the only one with a cherry stone still lodged between my teeth and my tongue.

"It was you, wasn't it? Bunch of ruffians, I know it was you! It's always you, no point denying it!" The greengrocer towered over us like a fairy-tale troll. "Open your mouths!" he bellowed. "Now!"

The Cursed One complied and stuck out her tongue, as did Filippo and Matteo. I could feel the hard surface of the stone inside my mouth and didn't even have the heart to breathe. Tresoldi got redder and meaner as he inspected Matteo's and the Cursed One's empty mouths: they must have licked their teeth clean of the red juice. He completely ignored Colombo's son, afraid to call him a thug, perhaps, to disrespect a name that couldn't be tarnished. Then he turned and looked at me.

"And you? If you don't tell me who stole my cherries, I'll tell your mother. And open your mouth right now if you know what's good for you!"

The Cursed One and the boys were looking at me, half-amused half-surprised, and frightened too, that fear that knocks the breath out of you. Her eyes shone like river pebbles in her solemn face. I didn't want her to think that I was afraid, that I wasn't good enough to catch fish with them by the river. I flattened my tongue against my lower teeth to gather more saliva, and swallowed.

Perhaps I'd die, bloated and livid, breathless. Perhaps that was what I deserved. Instead, I only felt the stone scratching down my throat and a feeble ache in my chest. Then, nothing. My mouth was clean and dry, and as Tresoldi yelled, "What the hell are you waiting for?" I threw my jaws wide open and stuck my tongue out, just as the Cursed One had done. He inspected us one by one, painstakingly slowly, then turned to face the square, perhaps searching for any witnesses who might seal our fate. I knew for certain that if we hadn't been surrounded by people on such a festive occasion, he'd have peeled our skin off like I'd seen him do with artichokes.

His fury had scarcely abated when he looked at me again: "Don't trust her," he said, pointing at the Cursed One, his face turning mean. "Stay away from her, or you'll end up with a cracked skull too."

3.

When they talked about her, it was always with a flick of the hand as if to swat away a wasp, or fingers darting to their mouths in fear to trace a cross. This was a little girl who'd barely started secondary school, and the adults talked about her like some kind of disease, or a rusty piece of iron, the kind that will give you a nasty cut and a fever and kill you.

At the park, I'd watch her as she walked through the gate, trying to push myself higher on the swings while my mother chatted with her friends, ensconced on a bench under the cedar trees, their hats and white gloves dappled by the sun streaming through the leaves. The Cursed One's mother never took her to the park. It was always her elder brother. Strong legs, large hands, dark hair, and factory soot lodged in the grooves of his face, Ernesto had just turned twenty. He cycled to town pumping on the pedals without ever touching the saddle, faster than the cars, even uphill. At the park, he'd sit away from everyone else, on the only bench entirely in the sun, and smoke his cigarette without saying a word, watching the Cursed One dangle from the oak branches and climb higher than everyone else.

When I'd asked why I couldn't swing from the trees with her, my mother had grabbed my wrist and told me I wasn't to go near the Cursed One: she was a jinx. Wherever she went, bad things happened—the kind of things my mother referred to as "calamities," in that low whisper she reserved for elegant, complex terms. The kind of things that happen to people who hang horseshoes the wrong way up, and instead of warding off accidents they bring them upon themselves. "Dangerous as the devil himself," my mother would say, with that southern lilt she had all but eradicated from her speech, because the other ladies would look down on her and stifle a giggle with their elegant, gloved hands.

"I don't believe you," I'd challenged her, "Why can't I be friends with her?" And so my mother had told me the story of the little boy who'd fallen out of a window and never got back up. It was one of those stories that traveled fast among mothers sitting in the shade, their chatter punctuated by the clacking of fans. One of those stories that fed on rehashed words and secret whispers.

It had happened one day, when the Cursed One was seven and was playing in the kitchen with her little brother, Dario, who was only four. Mrs. Merlini, her mother, had left them alone, just the time it took to borrow some salt from their neighbor. When she'd returned, Dario was nowhere to be found. She'd looked under the beds and in the wardrobes, in the laundry basket and behind the billowing curtains. Then she'd asked her daughter, who'd been standing there watching her the whole time: "Where is he? Where's your brother?"

She'd lifted her arm and pointed at the window.

"It wasn't my fault," she'd said.

Mrs. Merlini had poked her head out and looked down. Dario was in the courtyard, four floors down, glassy black blood oozing out of his mouth and ears.

4.

*M*y mother wanted me to be afraid of that scruffy girl so I wouldn't talk to her. That's why she'd told me about her little brother who'd fallen to his death and about her classmate who'd suddenly started yelling halfway through a dictation exercise, banging her forehead on her desk, over and over, until she'd toppled the inkpot and blood had spurted from her temples, froth gathering at her mouth. And about that time the wooden ruler a teacher had used to hit the Cursed One had snapped, embedding itself in the soft flesh between the teacher's thumb and forefinger as blood squirted all over the map of Italy on the wall. The wound had become infected, and the teacher had risked never being able to write on her blackboard again.

My mother hoped that those chilling, gory incidents would scare me away from the Cursed One, who'd surely end up putting the jinx on me, because that's what witches do. Those stories, however, had the opposite effect. I felt even closer to her: she, too, had had a younger brother who'd passed away, and maybe she, too, bore the guilt of surviving him.

My brother was not to be mentioned, my mother had decided. The only times we'd speak his name were on the Day of the Dead, and on April 26, when we'd deposit a bouquet of gladioli by the white tombstone at the bottom of the avenue flanked by plane trees.

When he was born, Mom had placed two tangerines and a bag of sweets wrapped in cheerful colors in his cot. "The stork brought a baby for us, and some treats for you," she'd explained.

But, even though the stork hadn't forgotten about me, I hated the baby all the same. He was too noisy, red, and flabby, and he couldn't stand on his own. He'd scream and wake us all every night, and my mother was always tired. She said I was like that too when I was little, but I didn't believe her. From the moment he'd arrived, I had ceased to exist.

I wasn't sad the day he died, and I had to squeeze the tears from my eyes so my parents wouldn't be upset. He'd turned the color of a ripe plum, and at some point he hadn't been able to breathe anymore, as if he'd swallowed a cherry stone that had got stuck in his throat. When the doctor said he couldn't be saved, my mother had gnawed at the bedsheets in desperation.

If someone had asked me to describe my mother, of one thing I'd have been absolutely certain: she was not happy. And she hadn't been even before the disease that had consumed the baby's lungs, the baby who'd been my brother for less than a year. In her rare serene spells, she'd recite lines from films she had seen at the picture house, or from plays, in her southern dialect. She'd throw open the wardrobes and put on her finest shawls, embellished with embroidered silk flowers and tassels. She'd show me old photo albums with tissue-thin, crinkly pages I wasn't allowed to touch for fear I'd rip them, and say, "Look at your mother. Look how beautiful she was." She'd tell me about women who weren't real women, but more real to her than my schoolteacher: Dido and Greta Garbo, Marlene Dietrich and Medea. All beautiful, all tragic. "I used to be like them," she'd say.

She met Dad at the Petrella theater in Naples when he was on holiday visiting his cousins and she was in a play, *Lo Sposalizio*. She enjoyed telling me how she'd let herself be charmed by that man with eyes the color of northern mist, a man she thought would make her a star. Now there was nothing left of those dreams, except for a lingering scent of tragedy. Her beauty had vanished. The plumpness she'd accumulated in her cheeks and belly so my father could have the children he wanted had remained lodged in her flesh, years after giving birth.

The doctors had decreed the seaside holiday was to blame, because that's where my brother had fallen ill with the disease that would paralyze his lungs until he drowned in his own body. After that summer when polio had devoured him, we'd never gone to the seaside again, and my father had insisted on holidaying in the mountains "to breathe some fresh air."

My mother retreated further into her own silences, absorbed in her self-imposed beauty regimes. She was on a strict diet and wore her hair fashionably short, crimped around the temples. Dad hated it. He said it was not proper for a woman to wear her hair short. Mom hid fashion magazines under their mattress—they were her Bible, her schoolbooks. Every day, she sat on the embroidered stool in front of the mirror, licking her fingers to test the temperature of her curling irons.

My father barely spoke to her. They were quiet and distant around each other, like two old dogs who'd lived in the same yard for years and had grown tired of each other's smell. There were days when he remembered he had once loved her—I could see it in the way he offered her his arm to help her down the stairs, or when he'd linger in their bedroom as she tied the ribbons on her dress, the smoke from the pipe hiding his face, hair thinning at the temples where his beloved fedora (which he wore on every occasion) had left a permanent mark. When he was nervous, he'd stroke his knuckles in ever-tighter circular motions. He was seldom at home, leaving in the morning without eating his breakfast and returning at dinnertime, hollowed out by the demands of the day at his hat factory.

There were only ever women in the house: myself, Mom, and the maids. Then the economic crisis had slowly crept up on us, the crisis Dad said had been caused by American banks. In March 1932 we had to move to a smaller apartment near Piazza Mazzini, and dismiss all the staff except for Carla, who constantly complained about her swollen legs and looked like a country bumpkin, but was cheap. Mom mended her own clothes and sat at her dressing table to keep up her "lady of the house" charade. Dad spent ever longer hours at the factory, his knuckles stroked to a polish, his absences fathomless voids.

I would hide in a closet and curl up where there was enough space, wedged between crisp shirts and soap bricks. I had to make sure the door was closed, only a thin slant of light penetrating from the outside, and then I'd bury my face in one of Dad's clean shirts and scream. Afterward, I'd feel better. But not for long. I had always enjoyed solitude, but the older I got, the more I realized that my life—far from expanding along with my body, my breasts, and my thighs—was instead shrinking, getting smaller and smaller, until one day I'd disappear.

Everything changed that day in June when, fearing I was going to die, I swallowed the cherry stone and looked at the Cursed One. It was the first time anyone had stared at me with eyes that seemed to say: "I have chosen you."

5.

*T*he following morning she showed up at my front door, in a dress a few sizes too big that slipped off one of her shoulders. She was pushing an old, rusty road bike with handlebars that curved like a sheep's horns. I stepped out on the balcony when I heard her calling: "You, Miss Cherry! Come over here!"

I was barefoot, nightgown floating around my ankles. She looked up, a hand slanted on her brow to shield her eyes from the sun.

"Hello!" she said, knocking her calf against the pedal.

"How did you know where I live?"

"I know a lot of things."

I kept staring at her, gripping the banister.

"Are you coming down or what?"

"What for?"

"To go to the river."

I hesitated. Then: "Together?"

"What d'you reckon I came here for?"

Behind me, I could hear the familiar noises of Carla tidying up in the kitchen, the quiet creaking of the sewing machine in the living room. My mother was singing an old Neapolitan song as if she was onstage. Dad had left while I was still asleep, leaving behind only the crisp smell of his tobacco that saturated curtains and rugs.

A streetcar clattered mere inches behind the Cursed One, blowing up her skirt, but she appeared not to have noticed: "Are you coming or what?" she bellowed above the rattling noise.

"My mother won't let me."

I could already hear her sneering "A good little girl only leaves the house to go on errands or to church."

"So don't tell her," she said instead.

I looked behind me, then back out toward the street. I could grab the curtain and slide down from the balcony, or climb down the drainpipe, or steal the keys from my mother's handbag and sneak out. I wondered what the Count of Monte Cristo would do, or the Black Corsair. But they remained quiet, hidden behind their book covers in my bedroom, tangled in their own adventures in faraway places. And there I was, on my balcony, in my nightgown. And I couldn't even climb a tree. And they were all boys, and I was nothing but a girl. And girls were meant to be rescued.

I looked at Maddalena and said, "I can't."

She scratched at the mark on her face as if it were an old wound that had started itching again, then shrugged. "Suit yourself." She turned the bike around, hopped on a pedal, and darted all the way down Via del Mercato bent over the handlebars, skirt billowing in the wind, without ever touching the saddle, just like her brother. She whisked between two huddles of housewives with their shopping bags, scattering them like pigeons, then disappeared behind the sturdy frame of a streetcar.

I went back inside, closing the window and drawing the curtains. In the living room, my mother looked up from her sewing machine, her foot coming to rest on the pedal: "Who was that?" she asked.

"No one."

"I should hope so," she mumbled approvingly, her attention back to the sewing machine. "You are far too young to have an admirer," she proclaimed to the red fabric stretched between her fingers. "You must take care to preserve yourself. You are not yet a woman, but be wary of boys all the same."

"I know," I said, even though I'd never really understood my mother's lectures on womanhood. One day I'd stop being who I was and become someone else, perhaps someone obsessed with manners, like her. A day charged with mystery, and shame, and fear.

I slid between the permanently parched potted plants—my mother never remembered to water them. Living things were the least of her concerns. I had to twist sideways to squeeze between the large briar-root sideboard and the claw-foot table that took up the entire dining room. Although the new apartment had only four rooms, my mother had insisted on keeping all our things, and as a result, the place—overrun with furniture, pewter figurines, copper pans, and carved statues of the Virgin Mary—felt like a cheap antiques shop. Every single object was, however, polished to a shine, not a speck of dust in sight.

I went into the kitchen and found Carla kneading something in a bowl, clumps of flour and butter stuck to her fingers. She was a strong, sturdy woman with a golden cross always shining on her chest and neat rows of clean teeth. She only charged thirty lira a week, but my mother was ashamed of her rough, grainy Bergamo accent and chunky legs.

"Why so sad, doll?" she asked, with that smile that lit up her face. I shrugged and shook my head. She pinched my cheek, leaving a smudge of flour on my jaw. "Go on, you can tell old Carla."

I remained silent, tracing circles in the mound of flour on the table. Carla drew a long breath, then got back to work. "Pass the

eggs, will you?" she reprised, jerking her chin toward the shelf by
the sink, where an egg carton sat next to the milk bottle and a bag
of flour. "And watch it, that's all we've got in the house!"

That's when I got the idea. "Here," I said, as Carla held out her
hand. But I let go a second too soon, and the eggs went crashing onto
the floor, soaking the carton.

"Ah, look what you've done! I told you that's all the eggs we had!
What do I tell your mother now?"

"I'll go fetch some more," I said, by way of an apology.

She frowned. "And since when are *you* so keen to be running
errands?"

I picked up the moist cloth that hung by the sink and crouched.

"Leave it. I'll take care of it," Carla snapped. "Go and get some
money for the eggs from your mother; the cake has to be ready for
lunchtime."

I went back to the living room and made for Mom's sewing machine, breath hitching in my throat as my bare feet sunk in the thick
rug. She only acknowledged me when I was inches away from her.
The pedal came to a halt and her eyes fixed on mine: "What now?"

"Carla says I have to go buy some eggs."

"Nonsense. Tell her to look in the pantry, they've just been delivered." She pumped her foot on the cast-iron pedal and stroked the
wheel to restart the machine.

I swallowed a lump of saliva and replied, "They broke."

"What do you mean they broke?" my mother snapped, banging
a hand on the worktop.

"It was me, ma'am. I'm so sorry." Carla peeked out of the kitchen
door, wiping her hands on the apron.

My mother's face hardened. Without saying a word, she stood
and made for the sideboard with the large mirror in the hallway,
walking slowly as she tugged at the belt of her dressing gown.

"How many times have I told your father?" she muttered, rooting for her purse in her ostrich-feather bag. "We should have kept Lucia, not Carla. She's a liability, this one. It's an outrage!" she concluded, unearthing the purse.

She slapped a five-lira coin emblazoned with the Fascist eagle in my hand. "Get a dozen while you're at it. Tell the greengrocer they're for Mrs. Strada, and there'd better be some change. And don't be long."

Before rushing to my room to get dressed, I glanced at the kitchen door. Carla stood on the threshold, looking at me. I mouthed a "thank you" and clasped the silver coin in my hand, guilt dripping down my back, slimy like raw egg white.

Outside, a scorching sun and not a breath of wind. The streets were teeming with people, sweat, chatter from the gaggles of matrons outside the shops, and the rattling of streetcars headed for the town center. I'd put on my favorite dress, the one with the oak leaf print, and the gold chain I'd got for my first communion. I skipped along Via Vittorio Emanuele, running my fingers through my hair. For the first time, I wanted people to point at me, say my name, whisper, "She's grown into a real beauty!"

I felt awkward walking by Tresoldi's shop and quickly strode past it, hunching my shoulders, a hand lifted to shield my face. Then I broke into a run. At the bottom of the street, two stone lions stared at me from the columns either side of the bridge, their paws crossed. I looked down from the parapet, scanning the pebbles and the river, which in that season was a narrow, dark strip of water. They were all there: Filippo stood with his feet in the Lambro, skipping a handful of stones on the water, his shoes abandoned on the bank with his bunched-up socks stuffed inside them. Matteo was wedging a large branch into the mud-streaked stones and the Cursed One sat peering into a tin watering can.

She was the first to spot me. She raised a hand and simply said: "Come down!" as if she'd been expecting me.

"How?"

She jerked her head toward a crumbled section of the embankment, overgrown with ivy.

"I can't get down from there!"

"Yes, you can." And she kept rummaging inside the watering can.

I turned and looked at the passersby, but nobody seemed to pay any attention to me or the other kids down by the Lambro. I crossed the bridge, keeping close to the parapet, which got progressively thinner, leaving enough room between the columns to squeeze through. I reached the collapsed section where the wall was missing a few bricks. If I treaded carefully, I could slot my feet into the thick snarls of ivy branches and lower myself down. But I'd never done anything like that, and from where I was standing, the drop was so big that if I fell, my head would surely crack open like an egg and there'd be no going back home afterward.

"Are you sure there's no other way?" I shouted.

Filippo and Matteo burst out laughing, then went back to their respective tasks as though nothing in this world mattered more than skimming stones on the river and digging in the mud with a stick. The Cursed One seemed to have forgotten about me. All I could see was her back, pointy shoulder blades peeking out of her dress.

I took a deep breath and started praying. I did it quickly and without promising Jesus anything in return—I wasn't asking for a miracle, after all, only not to fall, or at the very least, for the Cursed One not to turn around and laugh at me. I gripped the slim stone columns, dangling my legs from the bridge. I stretched one out as far as I could, but I couldn't reach the ivy branches. I flipped on one side, my back now facing the river, and started lowering myself down, feeling around blindly for a foothold. I took another breath, then looked down and felt nauseous. I relaxed my neck as the stench of mud and dark, murky water penetrated my nostrils.

When my feet finally touched the ground, my knees buckled. I stood, brushing dirt from my skirt. The Cursed One watched me trudge across the pebbles, and there was that smile again, the same as the day before when she'd stared at me on San Gerardino bridge. She stood, wiping her hands dry on her thighs: "I knew you were coming."

"Me too," said Filippo. The stone he threw bounced twice, ripples widening in the water, then sank.

"That's not true!" echoed Matteo.

"Yes, it is!"

"No, it's not." Matteo dislodged a large rock with his stick, uncovering wet, black soil teeming with worms.

"It's you who said she was too afraid to do it."

"And you said she was going to die for sure!"

"What do you mean?" I asked, heart pounding in my throat.

"He said that!" Matteo lifted the stick and pointed it at Filippo, flicking mud on his clean shirt.

Filippo tossed another pebble: "My father says if you eat a cherry stone, a plant will grow in your belly and come out of your ears and nose and then you can't breathe. Same as if you tell a lie."

The Cursed One must have seen the terror in my eyes, because she walked up to him and punched his shoulder. "Shut up! You know nothing."

Filippo whined like a dog, massaging the spot between his arm and collarbone and biting his lower lip. You could have stuck a finger between his top teeth.

"Whimpering like a girl!" sneered Matteo.

The Cursed One strode to him, grabbed the stick, and whacked him behind the ankles. He landed on his bottom with a stifled moan as she threw away the stick and turned to face me: "Are you coming with us then?"

"With you? Where?"

"I'll show you." She went to fetch the watering can, lodging it in the crook of her arm and lifting it effortlessly.

"What about the worms?" asked Matteo, jerking his chin toward the dark soil in the hole.

"We don't need any more," she proclaimed. "These will have to do." She bent over to pick up her sandals, tying the leather straps together, and flinging them over her neck. She started along the river, leaving the bridge behind, leaning on one side to balance the weight of the watering can. Matteo and Filippo followed her—one retrieving his shoes, the other the stick. Neither of them offered to carry the can for her.

I ran after her too and fell into step beside her. I felt out of place with my clean socks and shoes with a smooth sole, but I put on a confident voice, like hers, and asked, "What have you got in there?"

"Fish," answered the Cursed One. "But we only caught three today."

"And what do you do with them?"

"They're for catching lizards."

"The fish?"

"Yes."

"And what's fish got to do with lizards?"

"The fish are for the cats," she explained, as though she was having to point out that the sky was blue.

"The cats?"

"You'll see," she said, picking up the pace until all I could see was her back, the watering can knocking against her hip, and the wet footprints she left on the rocks.

We walked on in a silent procession, the Cursed One at the front, the rest of us a few steps behind. When she turned to make sure we were still following her, I could see the blemish on one side of her face—it ran from her temple to her ear and then all the way down to her chin. Dad had explained to me that it was called "angioma," which meant she had a disease under her skin. Mom said it was where the devil's lips had touched her, and it was a sin to even think about her. A disease and a curse at once, then—anybody else would have tried to hide that mark. Not her.

All around us, the Lambro and its residents went about their life. The noises frightened me: rats scuttling, ducks squawking, water dripping and reverberating in the musty darkness under the bridge. The Cursed One stopped as we reached what they called "the water-fall drop," the point where the riverbed crooked into a half-moon bend and water would froth and gurgle when the Lambro was full. Now, however, in the dry season, only tiny rivulets intersected the rocks. The Cursed One dropped the watering can and pointed straight ahead: there, where tufts of weeds grew in between the stones, were the cats. Some stretched on the scorching rocks, others stalked the tall grasses, hissing.

"Now watch this," said the Cursed One. She rolled up her sleeves and rummaged in the watering can, extracting a fish. Gripping it in her hand, she began cautiously padding toward the cats. I watched her bend over as she approached one of the cats, black as charred bread, gleaming white eyes, tail pointing upward. Between his jaws squirmed a fat, bright-green lizard. The Cursed One lifted the fish and offered it to the cat, who dropped the lizard and swiped his paw just as she threw the fish far behind him. The cat pounced and so did she, leaping into the grass.

"Look how big!" she shouted as she stood, a lizard writhing in her fist. She pinched the lizard's tail with her other hand and pulled it clean off. Holding it between her thumb and forefinger, she watched it curl around her fingers. Filippo and Matteo stuck their arms into the watering can. "I'll catch an even bigger one!" said Filippo, defiantly.

"Pffft! Yours always get away!" Matteo taunted him, laughing out loud as he lifted a fish. Filippo started panting, furiously rooting inside the watering can. Matteo and the Cursed One shot down the drop, elbowing each other, and you'd have had a hard time figuring out whether they were trying to capture lizards or get covered in cat scratches. They came back clutching fistfuls of lizard tails, stretching their arms out to count and compare their wounds. Filippo kept to one side, empty-handed, his shirtsleeves wet, kicking at the tufts of grass and scaring away the cats.

"And what do you do with those?"

"I collect them," answered the Cursed One as she stuffed the tails inside her pocket, "like trophies."

"And where do you keep them?"

"Under my bed. In a jar filled with vinegar." She ran two fingers over one of the scratches then sucked the fingertips. "Do you want to have a go?" she asked.

"I don't think I can do it."

"She's afraid. She's a *girl!*" said Matteo, spitting out that last word like a slimy chunk of gristle that you can't bring yourself to swallow. That's not what he called *her*.

"That's not true! I'm not afraid," I lashed out.

The Cursed One flashed me a cocky smile. "Then show me."

"Can't we play a different game?" I ventured, avoiding her stare.

"What game?" asked Filippo, who I gathered was not so fond of catching lizard tails either.

"I don't know. Something without lizards?" I shrugged. "Maybe we could pretend we're pirates and that's our ship?" I said, pointing at a large tree trunk that had fallen across the drop. "Like in adventure novels."

"No," ground out the Cursed One. And her face turned serious all of a sudden, eyes as cold as death.

"But why?" I asked, my mouth dry.

"Because I say so."

"We never pretend," explained Filippo, shrugging.

"And why not?"

"Because it gets dangerous," volunteered Matteo, toying with the lizard tails in his fist.

"Dangerous how?"

The Cursed One had lost all interest in me. Her eyes were fixed on a spot beyond the river, beyond the bridge, as if looking for something she'd lost. That's when the cathedral bells started tolling. I counted twelve strikes. Noon, and I hadn't got the eggs yet. Carla's cake wouldn't be finished in time for lunch and Mom would blame me. Or maybe Carla would be punished because of me.

"I have to go," I said, feeling for the coin in my pocket.

"Where?" asked Filippo.

"To get some eggs at Tresoldi's," I replied, swallowing hard. Fear gripped my stomach at the mere thought. "The ones we had at home . . . I dropped them so I'd have an excuse to get out," I continued, hoping for the Cursed One's approval.

She burst out laughing. "You dropped them on purpose?"

I gave a slight nod.

The Cursed One jerked her chin. "I'll come with you."

"Aren't you afraid?"

"Afraid of what?"

"Of Tresoldi. He'll remember you stole his cherries. He knows it was you."

"Me? I'm not afraid of anything."

6.

The bridge now behind us, we walked side by side along Via Vittorio Emanuele, me with my hands in tight fists inside my pockets, the Cursed One steering her bike, a foot balanced on one of the pedals. People turned to look at us. I wasn't used to those stares and felt dirty all over, but the Cursed One held her head high, seemingly unbothered.

"You're bleeding."

"So what?" She lifted her arm and licked the angry, raised welt that ran from her wrist to her elbow. "This way it'll heal quicker," she explained.

Tresoldi's shop was at the end of the street. I could see the shop sign, the advertisements for tomato paste, the windows made hazy by years of cursory wiping with water and old newspapers. The Cursed One propped her bike against the crates of fresh fruit piled by the door and climbed the three steps. "Are you coming?" she urged with an impatient flick of her hand, as if to say, I haven't all day.

I joined her and made myself walk in. A bell rang as we opened the door. The shop was warm and humid, an earthy smell of potatoes hanging about the place. I saw bottles of wine, tinned fruit and vegetables stacked on the top shelves. Balanced on an iron ladder by a row of Cirio preserves and a Mussolini calendar, suspenders dangling from his waist and a jar of strawberry jam in his hand, Noè spun around, sighing as he saw us.

"Coming!" we heard Tresoldi call from the back of the shop. He emerged from behind the frosted-glass door marked "Private." Noises floated in from the courtyard—a dog barking, geese honking. He wiped his fingers on a blackened piece of cloth, hobbling toward the counter, and stepped into the hazy light that filtered in through the shop windows. The backs of his large hands were crisscrossed by cuts from artichoke thorns, fingernails rimmed with dirt. His eyes narrowed into hard slits when he recognized us: "What are you doing here?"

An acrid tang invaded my mouth, like the sodium bicarbonate my mother gave me when I had an upset stomach. The Cursed One jabbed an elbow into my side. I swallowed my fear and began: "I need some eggs. One of the large boxes. I'm Mrs. Strada's daughter—she sent me."

"I know who you are," he replied, tossing the cloth over his shoulder. Then he pointed at the Cursed One: "And I know who this piece of work is too. Bag o' bones, but more cunning than the devil himself."

The word *devil* rattled me.

"She's got money," said the Cursed One, lifting her chin. "She'll pay for the eggs, so you have to give them to her."

I uncurled my fist and showed him the five lira coin. Tresoldi's eyes bored into us in a long, silent stare. I was certain he was going to smash our heads with the iron nutcracker that hung from a hook by the sack of hazelnuts. Instead, he ran his tongue over his front teeth and replied, "I don't sell to thieves, not even an apple core. If you steal from me once, I never forgive."

"And you—you stole the butcher shop from Mr. Fossati. Who forgave you?" blurted the Cursed One. Tresoldi snorted, pointing at the door:"Don't you dare come here again," he snarled,"or you'll get what's coming to you. I'll feed you to the geese!"

I ran out, breathless, my shoulders bent low, and the Cursed One followed, making a show of stomping on the tiles."Watch you don't step on your own tail, devil's spawn!"Tresoldi bellowed from inside the shop. We stopped at the bottom of the steps. She stuck her tongue out then turned to me: "Don't cry. It's no use. Crying is for idiots."

"I can't," I sniffed, wiping my tears with my sleeve. "Why did you say that?"

"Because it's true!" she snorted. "We can get the eggs ourselves, you know. We'll show him."

"Didn't you hear him? He said if we go back he'll feed us to the geese!"

"Only if we get caught." She smiled one of her mischievous smiles. Then her face crumpled.

"What's wrong?"

She pointed at the shop. I turned and saw Noè standing on the threshold, with those dark, tight curls of his, hair so big and thick I could sink both my hands in it and they'd never find their way out.

"What do you want?" asked the Cursed One.

Noè hesitated, then he joined us. "Here," he said, handing me a dozen eggs.

"Why?" I asked, clutching the carton to my chest.

He shrugged. "That's what you wanted, isn't it?"

"Thank you."

His chestnut eyes stared at mine and I flushed. I held out the coin but he shook his head: "I have to go back in or he'll get mad." There was a hint of a wave, a hint of a smile before the door closed behind him.

"Bye, then."

The egg carton was still warm and it smelled of him: an animal, feral smell mixed with dark tobacco. A scent I found I liked.

"I'm not sure we can trust him, you know," commented the Cursed One.

At home, I stared at my reflection in the mirror. My cheek was red where my mother had slapped me—she'd been waiting for me, and I'd been gone a long time. My dress was ruined too, my shoes dirty. "Where were you? Wretched girl!" she'd yelled at me. I hadn't answered. Now I was standing in front of the mirror in my underwear, gripping the edge of the sink, my sodden dress dripping from the rack over the bath. "Me? I'm not afraid of anything," I repeated, examining a pink, glossy graze on my upper arm. I must have got it when I lowered myself through the ivy and the collapsed bricks of the embankment. I was proud of my wound, but it was no match for the Cursed One's arms, covered in scratches. "Me? I'm not afraid of anything," I repeated again, my chin held high, hoping to catch a glimmer of her fierceness in my features, which I'd always considered dull.

On one side was life as I knew it; on the other, the life the Cursed One had shown me. What had once seemed right now appeared distorted, like seeing your own reflection in the water when you wash your face in the sink. In her world, scratches were badges of honor and pain could be licked away like blood. It was a world where you couldn't play games where you pretended to be something you were not, and you talked to boys looking them dead in the eye.

I was perched on the edge of this world, looking in, so close to slipping. And I couldn't wait to fall.

7.

*T*hat Saturday, Dad announced he had invited someone over for lunch, someone important. It was an exceptional occurrence, because Mom hadn't been keen to receive since we'd moved into the smaller house. She instructed Carla to walk slowly, keep her back straight and her lips sealed. And the food had to be perfect—tortellini soup (the broth had to be made from scratch with fresh cuts of meat and vegetables, not stock cubes, which were for misers) and then a joint of stuffed roast beef, which I found disgusting. Mom, for her part, wore the dress with the cinched waist that just about grazed her ankles, her pearl necklace, and diamond earrings. Then she unearthed a photograph of Mussolini from one of the drawers and positioned it in pride of place on the sideboard.

Dad's guest and his wife arrived late and didn't apologize. She crinkled her nose at the lace throw on the sofa, he wiped the mud from his boots on the rug. I recognized him from the arrogant way he looked at things, as if everything had been arranged especially for his pleasure, my mother included. Colombo brushed his lips over her knuckles and adjusted the badge on his coat. Although he'd never liked him or his car, Dad bowed and scraped: "Welcome, sir.

Please, take a seat." Mom had insisted Carla wear a uniform and cap: "If you embarrass us, I'll have your head!" she'd told her.

I had to sit up straight, elbows glued to my sides, napkin on my lap, and keep quiet "like a good girl" while the grown-ups discussed grown-up things and Dad laughed at something Colombo said. I had to smile, say "thank you" and "please," and speak only if spoken to. I had to sip the broth without making a noise and pick up the cutlery in the right order. Mom had never scolded me for getting a bad grade in school, but she had always insisted on table manners: she'd rather have a polished daughter than an educated one. There were so many rules that I'd lost my appetite. I sought comfort in Carla, who pulled faces at me behind my mother's back to make me smile.

I couldn't bring myself to eat the roast beef. It was piping hot, the stuffing green and mushy. Yet another rule, however, dictated that the plate couldn't be removed until it was empty. So I chopped up each slice into tiny morsels and quietly dropped them from the tip of my fork onto the napkin on my lap. Dad, meanwhile, gesticulated as he expounded on Flemish felt and braided tassels. Colombo nodded, pretending to follow even when Dad moved on to tacking and the different ways in which hats are shaped. "A true Fascist always keeps his word, Mr. Strada," he repeated. "I'll get you that deal." That was when I knew: to save his factory, Dad would have made a deal with the devil himself.

The men did nearly all the talking, my mother and Mrs. Colombo's conversation mostly confined to insignificant remarks on the color of the curtains, the perfectly polished silverware, and the intricate macramé embroidery on the tablecloth, which was part of my mother's trousseau.

Carla removed my plate. A hot, damp bundle oozed on my thighs. While my mother prattled on—"May I interest you in a digestif, Mr. Colombo? Mrs. Colombo, do try the pastries . . ."—I fumbled for an excuse to get up. "Please excuse me," I said as I pushed my chair back. "I need to use the lavatory." The napkin slid down my legs and landed with a wet thud on the floor. Carla, who was pouring the wine, stepped on it and briefly lost her balance. The bottle slipped from her fingers and tumbled onto the table, knocking over plates and glasses from "the good set" and flooding everything in red. Colombo shot up, his chest and legs dripping with wine, and yelled a bad word—one of those words that, if you said it even by mistake, would require ten Hail Marys and crossing yourself twice to make amends. Mom didn't say anything to Mr. Colombo. Neither did Dad. They looked at me. They looked at me like I was a severed lizard tail to be chucked in the river.

The following day I pretended to be ill. I woke early, before Carla could come in with her "Up with you, Miss Slugabed," and rubbed my forehead until I felt it warm under my fingers, then wiped my face with a cloth I'd soaked in boiling water. It was so hot it hurt. I walked to my parents' bedroom, barefoot, in nothing but my nightgown, and found my mother sitting in front of the mirror, testing the temperature of her curling irons with a wet finger. A sewing magazine lay half open on the dressing table—she had it delivered every month to stay up-to-date on the latest trends in womanly pursuits. Mom had wedged her rollers against the spine of the magazine to stop them sliding off. "Put your slippers on. Only tramps walk barefoot."

"I'm not feeling well," I said, rubbing my arms as if I had the chills.

She studied my reflection in the mirror. "Come over here."

I stepped closer. She moved the searing irons out of the way, grabbed my chin, and rested her lips on my forehead. "You're burning up," she said, "and you're all sweaty! See what happens when you go traipsing in the mud? I knew it!"

"I'm sorry."

"Enough. Get back to bed, I'll have Carla bring you a tonic," she replied, wrapping a strand of hair around the irons.

Dad was in the bathroom, his neck and chin white with shaving cream. "Aren't you ready yet?" he asked when he saw me walk back to my bedroom.

"I've got a temperature."

He hesitated, the lather dripping in large clumps onto the sink: "Does your mother know?"

I nodded.

"Very well." He tapped the razor on the edge of the sink, then ran it up his neck. "Excellent."

Carla was folding the cot she slept on and replacing it behind the sofa. "Do you want me to bring you something to eat?"

I shook my head and thanked her, faking a cough before I disappeared into my bedroom. I lay in bed, breathing, a hand resting on my heart, while I listened to the familiar Sunday morning noises: cups clinking in the kitchen, a shuffling of slippers soon replaced by Mom's heels clacking on the floor. "We're late," Dad was saying. "I can't find my bag," Mom replied. "And my hat, where's my hat? No, not that one, the one with the turquoise veil!"

They didn't come in to check on me.

As soon as I heard them leave, I sat up. I tugged my nightgown over my head and grabbed an old dress, one of those that languished at the bottom of the wardrobe for Mom to mend. The reflection in the mirror was an image of me I had yet to get used to, swelling in unexpected places, soft curves appearing on my hips and thighs. I had acquired two purple bruises on my bicep and calf which I was extremely proud of. I slipped on the old dress, which felt tight around the chest and beneath my arms. I didn't put my shoes on—they were firmly clasped in my hand as I tiptoed down the corridor.

Carla was tidying up the kitchen, crooning: *"Nell'amor si fa sempre cosí . . ."* She had the radio on. Dad only ever listened to important men giving speeches over in Rome, but when Carla was home alone, there was always music. When I reached the door, I'd been holding my breath for so long that I felt ill. As I pushed down the handle, a voice behind me teased: "Feeling better already? Must've been another miracle of Saint Alexander's!"

Carla stood there, fists framing her hips, and stared at me for a while. Then she burst out laughing: "What's his name then?"

As I fumbled for a reply, I realized I didn't even know the Cursed One's real name.

"Now listen here—he's not one of those sleazes who can't keep his hands to himself, huh? With a lamb like you?"

I figured Carla was referring to those things my mother always warned me about when she reminded me I was "just a girl," things I mustn't think about because it was a sin. Carla, however, probably thought there was no shame in what happened between boys and girls, it was all natural, but I was only a child.

"Noè," I blurted without thinking. "Noè Tresoldi."

Carla's eyebrows arched: "You better be back before mass is over, Missy," she said, "or I'm the one who's going to get into trouble!"

I sprinted all the way down Via Vittorio Emanuele, oblivious to the people in their Sunday best on their way to the cathedral, confident I wouldn't run into my parents: without me slowing them down, they were surely at the church already, Mom eager as always to secure the best seats. I stopped to catch my breath only when I got to the bridge, cheeks and calves on fire.

I leaned on the parapet—she wasn't there. There was only Matteo Fossati in his shorts, shirtless and barefoot on the rocks, bent over the water. He sank his hands into the river and hauled out his empty fists, swearing. I poked my head out from the collapsed section of the embankment and called him. He eyed me like a bad taste you can't banish from your mouth: "Might as well stay where you are. She's not coming today."

"Why?"

"What do you care?"

"Did she say where she was going?"

"If she says she's not coming, she's not coming, and that's that."

What could I do? Going home was not an option, the excitement of faking a fever and running to the bridge still coursing through my veins. The bells tolled. Eleven o'clock. With my eyes to the ground, I crossed to the other side of the bridge to check—maybe it was a joke, and the others were just hiding.

That's when I heard a screeching noise and shouting. Startled, I froze in the middle of the road: a black car bared its teeth at me. I saw my terror reflected in the gleaming metal of the front lights as a woman with a silk scarf tied around her neck leaned out the passenger side, yelling, "Are you *trying* to get run over?"

"Isn't that the Strada girl?" commented the driver, removing his hand from the horn and craning his neck out the window. "Does your father let you run around like a stray dog?" Colombo asked with an oily grin.

"Considering they teach her to keep her food scraps on her lap, I'm not surprised," quipped Mrs. Colombo. She examined me with cold eyes, and fear gripped me. Mrs. Colombo had always looked down on my mother, and she would relish the opportunity to humiliate her, revealing she'd seen me on the bridge, alone, in an old rag of a dress.

I stepped aside to let the car pass, all hot and bothered, thinking it would only take a word from them, a whisper during mass, for me to get caught. On the back seat I spied Filippo in his "Balilla" Fascist uniform, a tassel dangling from the black fez. He seemed ashamed to wear it. Next to him sat Tiziano, his elder brother, blond and pale like him, hair so heavy with pomade that it looked like a helmet, black shirt buttoned all the way up. The car resumed its climb on the way to the cathedral and Tiziano waved at me, while Filippo did his best to sink into the seat, covering his face with his hands. When the Cursed One was around, it didn't matter who your parents were, or what they'd taught you to believe, what they'd taught you to hate. It didn't matter that Matteo's father was with "the Reds" and Filippo's polished his Fascist Party badge and never passed a Mussolini portrait without saluting it with a raised arm. Without her, however, those two worlds were once again irreconcilable.

Maybe she'd actually fallen ill, and if only I knew where she lived I could go visit her, see if all those cuts on her arms hadn't become infected after all, and she was really dying. My mother said cats carried diseases in their claws, and if they scratched you they'd poison your blood. I sat on the pavement, hands fisting on my lap, clutching that terrifying thought.

"What are you doing sitting here like that?" Noè was looking at me from his bike, crates of fresh fruit secured to the rack, one side of his suspenders dangling on his thigh. "Well?"

"Nothing."

"Nothing?"

I shrugged.

"Fine," he said, straightening his back and pushing down on the pedal.

I stood. "Wait."

He put his foot back on the ground to balance his bike.

"I don't know where to find her," I ventured.

"You do know everyone says you should stay away from her?"

"I know."

"And you don't care?"

"I don't care."

He burst out laughing. "I know where she lives."

"Really?"

"Sometimes I do deliveries there. She's on Via Marsala, near the Singer factory. Before the redevelopment she lived on the fourth floor of an old block of apartments in Sant'Andrea, but then they knocked all the houses down." He patted the crossbar: "I'll take you."

"Now?"

"Now."

I'd never done anything like that before: sitting on a boy's bike, balanced on the crossbar. That was something a girlfriend would do.

"All right," I replied, and he helped me up.

I gripped the handlebars with both hands and Noè started pedaling, arching his elbows and knees to make room for me. "Hold on tight!"

My stomach was in knots, heavy although I hadn't eaten breakfast. Sweat trickled down my neck and beneath my arms as the crossbar bit into my thighs. Noè climbed effortlessly all the way up to the cathedral, never touching the saddle, skirting around people out for a walk. When we got to the train station he sat back on the saddle, his legs grazing my hips. I'd never been to that part of town beyond the station, where the suburbs began, but most importantly I'd never been that close to someone, and I didn't know what to say. Luckily, he was silent, his attention focused on the road. I felt his collarbones pressing down on the nape of my neck, my hair brushing against his chin. His cheeks were ever so slightly rough, a hand-rolled cigarette tucked behind his ear.

"Here we are," he announced, although I'd stopped paying attention to where we were going. I watched as the tendons on his forearms tensed under his skin and I breathed in his scent of hard work and tobacco. Peeling my eyes from his arms, I let them wander over my surroundings: the tower blocks on Via Marsala were tall and straight, with long balconies and identical square windows, like those you'd see on a ship. Opposite them sat the new Singer factory, which had opened two months before, quiet and imposing behind the closed gates covered in large posters advertising sewing machines.

"That's the door," said Noè as he helped me down. "She's on the sixth floor."

"You're not coming?"

He cracked a smile, revealing beautiful teeth. "I've got deliveries to take care of," he replied, his thumb flicking to the crates of fruit on the rack.

I'd never seen him smile in his father's shop.

"Will you know how to get home afterward?"

"Yes," I lied, not wanting him to think I was a stupid little girl.

He pushed on the pedals and darted off before I could thank him.

I'd never been so far from home on my own, and that part of town, all shadows and vertiginous buildings and empty streets, seemed to weigh me down. People's voices and cooking smells wafted out from the windows, wide open against the heat. There was no concierge booth in the lobby; the front door was open. I looked around for someone I could ask for permission to come in, but there was nobody. I climbed all six floors, pausing to catch my breath on the landings crowded with bicycles, the stench from the lavatories at the end of the corridors drifting all the way up the stairwell. I recognized the Cursed One's rusty bike with its curved handlebars, resting against the railing—that must be her apartment. A brass plate on the door read "Merlini."

I paused, hand midair, counting my breaths. I told myself I'd knock on the count of ten, but I always seemed to lose track and start over again. A burst of laughter came from the other side. I gathered up my courage and knocked, feebly at first, then harder. The laughter stopped, and I heard someone say, "Maddalena, go and see who it is."

I held my breath. Hearing steps approaching, I considered running away. Suddenly I was afraid I had the wrong apartment, and a stranger would answer the door. Or worse, that I had the right apartment, but she'd turn me away.

The door opened and the Cursed One stood before me in a light dress, barefoot. Her face was clean, hands clutching ivory ribbons and scraps of lace.

"What are you doing here?"

"So that's your name," I muttered. "Maddalena—it's a beautiful name."

"What have you come here for?" she grimaced.

"I didn't see you at the river. I thought you might be ill and . . ."

"I'm never ill," she cut in. "You shouldn't have come looking for me."

A male voice called out from inside the house: "Maddalena, who is it?"

I stepped back and turned, ready to bolt.

She snorted. "Now that you're here, you might as well come in."

I followed her down a narrow hallway with bare walls that led to a small, bright room. In a corner I spied a lacquered cooking range with an iron stovetop and a little door where a fire burned. A crucifix and a portrait of the Virgin Mary hang on the wall next to a small tin-rimmed blackboard: "What are we missing today?" read the sign at the top. Someone had scribbled "Everything" underneath in white chalk. Further down, in a different handwriting: "But above all, milk." Old photos and a dry olive branch were tucked into the corners of the cupboard, wedged between the wood and the glass panes.

And in the middle of the room, standing on the dining table, was a young man wearing a bridal gown, work pants and black socks peeking out from underneath the lace. The hem came down to his calves, and his head brushed against a bare light bulb dangling from the ceiling. "Hello," he said, waving at me.

Two girls sat on straw-topped stools on either side of the table, which was covered in fabric swatches, pincushions, and tape measures. They were tacking the hem of the gown. One of them wore lipstick and her dark hair in a bob with a little curl on her cheek. She had Maddalena's black eyes. "Stop fidgeting or I'll have to start over!"

The other girl—beautiful locks tumbling down her shoulders, full bosom, glasses, a tape measure curling around her neck—stuck the needle into the fabric gathered on her knees. "Thank goodness we're not in a hurry," she commented, wrapping a piece of white thread around her finger and snapping it off with her teeth.

"But we can only work on this on Sundays . . ." complained the girl in the red lipstick.

I recognized the young man in the bridal gown. It was Ernesto, Maddalena's brother, the one who accompanied her to the park to climb trees, the one who'd been working at the Singer factory for a month. He had strong arms and soft features, dark, mussed hair, and impossibly long eyelashes casting shadows over his cheekbones.

I'd never seen the girls, however. Later I learned they worked on commission for Mrs. Mauri, the modiste, who had a shop in town. The one in the red lipstick was called Donatella and was Maddalena's older sister, the other was Luigia Fossati, Matteo's older sister, who had been engaged to Ernesto since March; they'd be getting married in the winter. She'd been staying up late for months, lining hats, sewing buttons, and mending elegant coats for other people's fancy trips, trying to save enough for two train tickets and a room in one of those big hotels in Nervi. They wanted a room with a balcony where they could spend a week looking at the sea and sipping coffee in the sun like rich people did. She only had Sundays to work on her own gown, and Donatella had offered to lend a hand. Ernesto had been pressed into service as a model because he was roughly the same height as Luigia and had wide hips like a woman's. Or maybe just because it was fun.

Maddalena introduced me. I have no idea how she knew my name—I certainly had never told her. She said I was a friend of hers and I felt proud and scared to be considered as such. The truth was, I had never had any girlfriends.

I bobbed a small curtsy. "Lovely to meet you."

Ernesto apologized for his current attire and the girls giggled. Donatella commented that Maddalena never invited anyone over, perhaps she was ashamed of them. The Cursed One scowled and folded her arms across her chest.

"Well, you can't blame her really, considering what you have me wearing!" quipped Ernesto. His laughter was like church bells on a wedding day.

"Will you stop laughing—I'll never get the hem straight," Donatella scolded him, holding the needle between her index finger and thumb as she wetted the thread on her lips and ran it through the eye of the needle. Luigia was looking at Ernesto with stars in her eyes, her mouth open in a full-bellied laugh.

"I thought it was bad luck for the groom to see the gown before the wedding," I said.

"Oh, it doesn't matter—he'll marry me anyway. Can't change his mind now!"

"That's why they're dressing me in skirts, so I can't run off!"

They offered me a pastry from a little golden cardboard tray on the sideboard and I said I needed to use the lavatory first. It was on the landing, so Maddalena accompanied me and waited outside.

I stepped in, pinching my nose at the stench. There was no water closet, only a ceramic-encased hole on the ground, with two small steps to rest your feet on. There was no cord to flush either, only a battered broom and old newspapers hanging from a hook. I closed the door—there was no latch, no lock. On the inside of the door, someone had scribbled: "Do try and hit the bull's-eye, this is no pigsty."

"Such a lovely house," I said, coming out.

Maddalena's lips curved in a bitter smile. "And what do you know, rich girl?"

She guided me to the kitchen sink to wash my hands with a large brick of Marseilles soap, the smell reminding me of a laundry room. Luigia and Donatella were helping Ernesto out of the bridal gown, ever so slowly, so as not to mess up the tacking. They draped it over the back of a chair, Luigia trailing the tips of her fingers over it, then we all sat around the table to eat the pastries as the scent of vanilla filled the room.

"We should be waiting until after lunch really, but they smell so good . . ."

"Leave one for Mom!" snapped Donatella, swatting Ernesto's arm away as he reached for his third beignet. They were celebrating. Although he'd only started work a month ago, the Singer job paid well, and soon it would be paying better still: Ernesto was going to be promoted to foreman. He'd already been looking into renting an apartment and had found a nice place on Via Agnesi, just two rooms, but light and airy. With Ernesto's salary and Luigia's earnings, they could afford to do it up nicely, maybe even get an icebox if they were careful with money.

"Hurry and start making babies, so you'll get lots of money from Mussolini!" Donatella teased. Luigia blushed, her lips dusted with icing sugar.

"He can give us a million lira for all I care. I don't want anything from *him,*" replied Ernesto.

"Oh, enough of your sermons!" Donatella grumbled. "When will you ever see that kind of money otherwise, huh? A little extra cash never hurt nobody. You'll get your Luigia a nice house, she deserves it . . ."

"He'll get the house, same as he got the pastries," Maddalena cut in, "He doesn't need anybody's help, you know?" She'd stopped eating, and an offended look settled on her face.

It fell to Ernesto to lighten the mood. He opened the windows and pulled the curtains aside so music from a radio in a nearby apartment could float in, together with the heat. He made us dance, one by one, to arias by Beniamino Gigli and popular songs by De Sica. I was stiff as a broomstick, but Maddalena nimbly executed all the steps. All it took was Ernesto's laughter and unyielding good humor for her anger to subside. When Luigia's turn came, he held her flush against him and they swayed to the music, foreheads touching, eyes closed, fingers interlaced.

And I envied them that house. It was small and the walls were bare, but it was a house you could dance in.

At the first notes of *"Parlami d'amore Mariù,"* someone turned up the volume.

"Oh, I really like this one!" said Maddalena, grabbing my hand. "No, not like that. Follow my steps."

I couldn't. My legs felt jointless, like a doll's, and I didn't know what to do with my arms.

She wrapped her hands around my waist then made me take off my shoes and step on her feet, even though she was shorter than me and I had to hunch my back to keep my balance. She was so close I couldn't breathe. I could smell her soap on me. My heart thumped in my chest, her clammy palm on my lower back gave me shivers.

She laughed as she sang about not wanting this to be a dream. She'd already forgiven me for turning up uninvited to her house.

The door opened and a gust of air slammed the windows closed, the music now a distant echo from behind the glass panes. Donatella wiped her lipstick off with a napkin and Luigia slowly peeled herself off Ernesto, tidying her hair. I hurried to slip my shoes back on, easing my heels in with my forefinger.

A woman in clogs and a black cotton dress walked in. "Onions are up again. Eighty cents per kilo. And three lire for beans now! Madness! If this goes on much longer you'll have to be made of money to go to the market!" she grumbled as she dropped the shopping bags on the table. "What's this? The table's not set yet? Sitting around eating pastries, are we?"

"We'll do it now, Mom."

"Leave it. You worry about the shopping. And tidy up this mess, the house's a dump!"

She gestured at Ernesto, then Luigia, then at the scraps of fabric strewn across the table: "Nothing like love to turn your brain to mush!" she snorted.

I didn't like Mrs. Merlini. She was bloodless as a slaughtered lamb on Easter Sunday, and looked at me with pale-blue, bulging eyes that seemed to cut right through me. She didn't introduce herself or ask me anything. I watched her drag her yellow, doughy body around, looking like she'd been molded off a brick of soft soap. My mother said you could always tell a lady by what she wore under her skirt, and she was careful never to ruin her silk stockings. Maddalena's mother's legs, however, were bare.

"Would you like to eat with us?" Luigia asked as she washed the dirt off the vegetables.

I searched for a clock and located one by the window. I hadn't realized it was already forty minutes past noon. "I'm sorry, but I really must go now." I thought of Carla, who was surely waiting for me, biting her nails. "Thank you for the pastries, and for everything else."

The mother spread an oilcloth over the table and began setting plates and glasses, staring at me with those eyes that saw right through me. She set the table for four, as though she'd forgotten someone. It was Ernesto who fetched an extra bowl and glass from the cupboard, without a word, seemingly used to his mother's forgetfulness. I studied the pictures wedged in the corner of the cupboard: there were a few saints' icons, photographs from weddings and first communions, and a portrait of a child who must have been about three, wearing a little sailor's hat. Maybe that was him—the brother who'd fallen out of the window.

"Did we settle the shop bill?" asked Donatella, filling a jug of water and placing it in the middle of the table. "The deadline was today."

"Ernesto went round after the 7 a.m. service," replied the Cursed One.

"Well, did someone go?" the mother asked again, brushing past Maddalena as if she hadn't seen her. "I don't like debts, you know."

"Yes, I did," confirmed Ernesto, then he went to stand by the sink to help Luigia with the vegetables. The mother placed four spoons and four napkins on the table. Donatella discreetly supplied the missing items.

"Why does she behave like that?" I whispered, stepping closer to Maddalena.

"Like what?"

"Like you don't exist."

"One day she said I wasn't her daughter anymore and started behaving like this," she answered with a shrug. She was speaking normally, not caring that her mother might hear her. "She used to howl and cry. And bash her head against things. It's better now."

I pointed to the picture wedged in the cupboard, the one of the little boy in the sailor's hat, and whispered again: "Is it because of him? Because he fell from the window?"

Maddalena's eyes hardened. "You know nothing."

"I'm sorry . . ." I tried to apologize, but she didn't give me time.

She grabbed my wrist and dragged me down the hallway, then opened the door and pushed me out.

"My mother told me about the accident, I didn't know . . ."

"It wasn't an accident," she cut in icily. "And that time my father lost a leg at the workshop and then the infection killed him—that wasn't an accident either," she continued, her face coloring red. "It was my fault. I make bad things happen. They told you that too, didn't they?"

"Maddalena, I'm sorry . . ."

"Don't call me that!" she hissed, looking like she'd just chewed on a poisonous berry. "They're right to tell you to stay away from me. If you don't, something bad's bound to happen."

My hands fisted until I felt my nails biting into my flesh.

"I don't care what other people say!" I blurted out. Then I turned my back to her so she wouldn't see me cry and wiped my face with my arm, running down the steps.

"Francesca!" the Cursed One called out. I'd already cleared two flights of stairs but I froze, my hand clutching the banister. She was looking down at me, her hair gathering like curtains around her forehead. "Are you coming tomorrow?"

I hesitated, sucking on my lip: "I thought we weren't friends any-more," I replied.

"Why not?"

I rocked on my heels on the step. "And where am I supposed to go?"

"To the river," answered the Cursed One. "I'll teach you to catch fish."

8.

*T*he following months went by in a flash in what was the happiest summer of my life.

I was getting good at telling lies, and with Carla's help I managed to sneak out to the river almost every day to be with the Cursed One and the boys, feet in the water, bare legs streaked with mud. I'd learned to only ever wear the same dress, the old faded one that I'd bunch up at the bottom of the wardrobe once home. Then, at night, while everyone slept, I'd wash the dirt away and hang it to dry outside my bedroom window. At home I wore long-sleeve blouses despite the heat to hide the scratches on my arms, and I softened the scabs on my knees with water and soap so they'd heal faster.

All those precautions were, as it turned out, completely unnecessary. Dad was so preoccupied with the deal Colombo had promised him that he barely left the factory, and the acrid smell of his tobacco had begun to fade from the house. I'd always known I couldn't compete with his job—his hat presses and machinery, his felt and his buckles: they would always be worth far more than me. But since the wine accident during that lunch that was meant to impress and instead turned into a disaster, I'd been wary of his apprehensions, of the way he'd taken to ignoring me. Perhaps, because of me, the deal would fall through, and my father would hate me forever.

Mom, by contrast, was happy and I couldn't understand why. The only thing she seemed to pay any attention to was the red dress on her sewing machine. She sang often in her melodious dialect, and at times even forgot to scold Carla for leaving a smudge on the cutlery or not folding the fitted sheets correctly. She was distracted. In the afternoon, she'd spray a few drops of lavender perfume behind her ears and leave on "urgent errands." She'd be out for hours, coming back with an empty shopping bag and mussed hair, then retreat to her room until dinnertime. Her indifference extended to me as well, but seeing as it afforded me more freedom, I didn't care. I took advantage of it and stole out to the river to catch fish with the Cursed Ones, to see who could find the oddest shapes in the clouds, to feel the sun scorch my skin until it flaked off.

And even when I didn't make it to the river, the truth is I couldn't escape Maddalena. I thought about her all the time, even in ways I was ashamed of: I imagined her rescuing me from the top floor of a burning building, or carrying me away from a battlefield, cradling me in her arms, bombs going off around us, blood everywhere, or again watching me twirl in my dress and telling me I was beautiful. But I kept all those flights of fancy to myself.

For some reason I was yet to understand and didn't dare ask about, pretend play was dangerous for Maddalena. The games she came up with were always made of dirt and breakneck sprints, climbs and jumps and daring escapes, and we were only ever ourselves, because playing at being other people and making up stories was forbidden. I, on the other hand, would have given anything to live in a world of pirates and heroes, where nobody talked about money or darning socks, where you sacrificed your life for the motherland or some other grand ideal, where women were always in "mortal danger," and if you died you died to save others, rescuing them at the last minute, and then you kissed at the very end, giving up the ghost on the lips of your beloved. And so sometimes, without telling anyone, when we ran in the dry riverbed or fought with sticks, I pretended to be someone else. I'd steal furtive glances at the Cursed One and copy the way her shoulders moved when she ran, the way she said, "I'm not afraid."

There was never a dull moment with the Cursed Ones. We'd wander around town barefoot, sneaking inside buildings to ring the bell, which sometimes involved turning a small mechanical key. If it was too hot, we'd go and bathe in the "frog fountain" in Piazza Roma, behind the redbrick building with gray stone pillars that had once housed the town council and was universally known as *Arengario*. We liked that fountain because it had a large marble basin so deep you could stand in it, and in the middle was a bronze statue of a girl crushing a frog in her hands, surrounded by a chorus of water-spouting frogs. We'd position ourselves each under one of those frogs, our mouths open to gather the water, and then spit it out as far as we could. If the carabinieri turned up, we'd bolt, laughing.

We'd ride to the park, although we only had two bikes: Maddalena's rusty one with the curved handlebars, and Filippo's, as shiny as the ones you'd see on the Giro d'Italia. He'd secured an old postcard to the rear wheel with a peg, so if you pedaled fast enough the bike sounded like a moped. I'd sit sideways on the Cursed One's bike, the crossbar biting into my thighs and her breath tickling the back of my neck. "Faster!" I'd urge her, my skirt bunched up in my hand so it wouldn't get caught in the wheels. When I was with her I wasn't even afraid to get hurt. Nine times out of ten we'd beat the boys to Villa Reale Park, where we'd lie on the lawn, ignoring the "Do not tread on the grass" sign, eat black bread and lard, and drink from the water fountains.

We enjoyed everything that scared us: the dark corners on the banks of the Lambro where the rats hid, the greengrocer cursing in the back of the shop, the floor creaking under his uneven steps. Now that I was with those kids I'd always watched from afar, it felt like the world began right there. Like my life had restarted from scratch.

In the end, I managed to hold my own in the lizard tail game and earn my fair share of cat scratches. It was just Maddalena and me that day. We chased the lizards and scuffled with the cats, then lay on the ground, our arms stretched on the sun-warmed rocks next to the severed tails we'd amassed, and compared our cuts, all red and swollen, glistening with droplets of blood. Maddalena pinched her skin to squeeze the blood out.

"Gross!" I said, but then I did the same, to show her I wasn't put out.

"Us girls mustn't think blood is gross," she said.

"Why?" When it came to boys and girls, I never understood anything people said to me.

I was afraid of boys, even Filippo and Matteo, whom I'd got to know a little, and Noè, with that strong smell I liked. It was my mother who taught me to be afraid of them: she said boys were beasts. "They will eat you alive, Francesca," she warned me, and I thought of the dog in Tresoldi's backyard, old and hoarse, choking on his chain all day to bolt at anyone who happened to walk by, straining to rip their throats out.

In Maddalena's world, there were no boys and girls—except she'd said, "*Us girls* mustn't think blood is gross." When I asked her why, she shrugged. "When we're older, we'll get it and there's no getting round it."

I pretended to understand, not wanting to feel like I was less than her. But the truth is that it troubled me, this blood we'd have to contend with when we got older, and I didn't even know where it was supposed to come from. Maybe from our eyes, like the statues of the Virgin Mary that cried blood, or from our ears and mouths like Maddalena's brother, who'd fallen out of a window and cracked his skull.

"I win!" said Maddalena. The blood had trickled down to the hollow of her elbow and between her fingers. She licked it off her knuckles and the palm of her hand as if it was cherry juice.

"Next time I'll win!" I retorted. But I knew I wouldn't. She was the one who enjoyed pulling the blind cat's tail, the meanest, the one who'd clamp his fangs on you the moment you touched him. She'd patiently stroke his belly while he furiously clung to her, head and paws, hissing and scratching and biting without quarter. As for me, I'd jump back as soon as the claws came out.

"Next time," she said. Then she crawled on the rocks until her face was hovering over my arms, grabbed one of my wrists, and began licking at the scratches. "They'll stop hurting quicker like this." We lay on our backs, the sky shifting before our eyes as shadows crept along the riverbank.

That's when she told me she didn't think they'd let her go back to school. She'd failed the previous year because of her bad behavior. It was her mother who didn't want her to go back—she'd told Ernesto those like her were better off finding a job, and fast, to bring home some money, and enough of her antics. If her mother had got her way, she'd have been sent to a trade school, never to a *liceo*, a school that was meant to prepare you for university. Ernesto, however, had insisted she should pursue her studies. "It's the only way you'll be able to defend yourself against this world," he maintained. That's the reason he wanted Maddalena to stay in school, in a *liceo*, although it was mostly rich people who sent their kids there. If they let her go back, we'd be in the same class, and every night I prayed that God would grant me that kindness. All that time without her—I couldn't stomach the idea.

"He said he'd pay for my books and everything else, and that I have to stay in school at all costs."

"You cannot not go to school—it's the law."

"If you've no money, then the law counts for nothing. But Ernesto says he'll take care of that."

"And what did you say?"

"I told him—I swore it to him—that they wouldn't make me repeat the year again for bad behavior," she explained, twirling a green lizard tail between her fingers.

"Why did they make you repeat the year?"

She hesitated. "I punched Giulia Brambilla. Gave her a huge bruise. She spat a tooth out too. So she went to the headmaster's—well, first to the school nurse, then to the headmaster's, but either way. She was crying, and they believed her and never even asked me a thing."

"But why?"

"Because she's a coward, that's why."

"I meant, why did you punch her?"

Her eyes narrowed as she looked at me. "She told everyone I pushed him."

"Who?"

She bit her nail, spat it out, then picked up the lizard tail again. "Dario. My brother. The one who fell."

I didn't reply at first. Then I turned on my side to face her. "So . . . how did it happen then?"

"He fell."

"He just fell?"

"He just fell."

"And why did you say it was your fault? Do you feel guilty that he died and you're still alive?"

Suddenly she turned away. "And what do you know about that?"

"I had a brother too."

She spun back. "And he died?"

"He didn't fall. Polio took him. He couldn't speak yet, he just . . . made a lot of noise. And before he died he made even more, as if he was trying to scream it all out, that thing he had lodged in his lungs. Then, nothing. We bring flowers to his grave, and Mum makes me light candles."

The Cursed One stuffed the lizard tail in her pocket and said, "So it wasn't your fault then."

"No," I lay back down, shut my eyes against the sun, and told her something I'd never told anyone before, something I knew would send me straight to hell: "When he died, everybody was sad. But not me—I couldn't be. I felt like I started breathing again the moment he stopped."

Maddalena was completely silent. Around us I could hear the river and the distant meowing of cats. I never should have told her. Now she'd tell me to go away, that I was a monster, a rabid dog that should have been clubbed to death.

"It happens," she blurted out.

"What happens?"

"To think of things that you can't speak about. Wrong things. Evil things. Doesn't mean you're evil too."

That secret burned me, weighed me down, crushed me. I felt sick. "He was innocent. He was just . . . living. Never even had the time to sin once. And I hated him." I took a deep breath and sat up. "You're the first person I've told. If people knew, they'd treat me differently."

The Cursed One had sat up too, chin resting on her knees, and she studied me with her grave, rock-hard eyes. Mine fixed on a drop of blood swelling from a cut on my forearm. "They'd start looking at me the way they look at you."

9.

*B*efore we knew it, September was upon us. That Sunday, the 8th, the Autodromo hosted the Grand Prix—an important celebration for the town. And as for all celebrations, the streets were decked in Italian flags: everywhere they hung from balconies and windows, garrets and gables. You didn't have to be a Fascist to hang a flag, but if you didn't you were *anti-Italian*, which was worse than having scabies. That day, however, the tricolor wasn't flying for some Fascist Party grandee, but for Tazio Nuvolari and his Ferrari Alfa Romeo, the only man who could beat the Germans and reclaim the title.

We'd gone to the early morning service because Mom wanted to enjoy all the events that had been planned. She'd been talking about it since the night before, when she'd dug out our flag, which stank of mothballs, from one of the sideboard drawers. She'd laid it out to air on the sofa, so it would lose the creases from the last time it had been ironed. That morning, before she even got out to buy a block of ice from the iceman, Carla had secured it to the railing on our balcony. The noise of revving engines over at the Autodromo could be heard all the way into our house, so strong it rattled the windows.

There was to be a rally and a parade, and the formal summons had been delivered to every family the previous week, in the shape of a card signed by the local party representative: "The authorities will be proud to attend the celebrations planned for the event, which will not fail to attract jubilant crowds of passionate supporters."

Children were going to take part in the parade too: the *Balilla* boys would lead, and us girls, the *Piccole Italiane*, were to march behind them in the square outside the cathedral. We'd be carrying the black and white checkered flag that signaled the end of the race, for it to be blessed by the archpriest. I'd been chosen, together with another girl, to recite the *Decalogo della piccola italiana*, the ten commandments all good Fascist girls must adhere to, and I was secretly very proud. I'd be stepping on the purpose-built stage, surrounded by all those "important people" my father always talked about. And in the end, I didn't really care that my skirt was too tight and my white cotton blouse too heavy, or that it pinched the flesh under my arms.

My mother made me stand on a chair in the living room and started fussing with my uniform, tucking the blouse deep inside my panties and smoothing the pleats of the black skirt. Then she handed me my white gloves, reminding me not to lose them.

"Aren't you coming?" she asked my father, who sat in his armchair smoking, hand cupped around his pipe.

"I'd rather not. I can't stand cars. Too noisy."

"People will talk."

"Let them talk," he snapped, his gaze on the potted plants on the balcony.

"As you wish," replied my mother, turning her back to him.

"Let's go!" she continued, grabbing my hand and forcing me to jump down from the chair, soles clacking loudly on the floor.

My father had never been a die-hard Fascist, one of those who traced a cross on their forehead every time they walked by a portrait of Mussolini, or chanted *"Eia, Eia, Alalà"* at the Saturday rallies. He'd joined the party purely out of self-interest—because being a member was good for business, everybody knew that. He'd join a ladies' gymnastics or sewing club if it helped sell more hats. At times, when he read the papers or listened to the radio, I'd hear him grunt or make unkind comments, but he'd long got used to restricting his concept of freedom to what could be done without attracting undue scrutiny, and to call people he secretly despised "friends." If he could at all help it, however, he shunned official celebrations and parades. Mom, by contrast, would always doll up, caught in the solemn atmosphere around town. She'd teach me how to hold my fingers and elbow straight for the Fascist salute. "We are part of something bigger," she'd explain, "and we must look our best."

That day she'd powdered her face singing the aria *"Casta Diva."* The previous night she'd hung her red dress in the wardrobe, the one she'd been working on all summer, gently stroking the fabric before going to bed. Now she wore it proudly as we dove into the swiftly flowing crowd headed for the main square—it felt like the whole town had poured onto the streets. Mom's boat-neck collar was trimmed with gold thread, her calves wrapped in silk stockings, men's eyes skating all over her. Nuvolari and his Alfa Romeo were plastered on every wall—he looked like a warrior prince on his steed from a fairy-tale book, but drawn in strong diagonal lines to give the illusion of speed.

Anticipation and heat weighed on the square. The men carried their jackets on their arms and fanned themselves with their panama hats, the women had clustered in small groups in the slither of shade provided by the roofs.

"I see Mrs. Mauri," Mom said. "I have to speak to her about a hat that needs mending. Go and join your friends, like a good girl."

"But . . . will you be watching when I'll be on stage?"

"Of course I'll be watching. Run along now." She let go of my hand. I watched her red dress being swallowed by the throngs of

people before I summoned up the nerve to join the other kids
in their black and white uniforms, already lined up outside the
church like a well-trained flock of swallows. I stood on my toes and
craned my neck, looking for Maddalena. She didn't usually care for
rallies and parades, because that meant rising early and squeezing
into her uniform, which was too tight, but she'd said she'd be there
that day: Ernesto loved cars, and he always watched the Grand Prix
from his favorite spot right behind the most dangerous chicane in
the racetrack. He wanted to feel the air whoosh past his face as the
cars sped by only inches from him, so fast his hat would blow off,
be deafened by the roar of the engines and the shouting from the
crowd, and breathe in the heady smell of gasoline and the excitement of the race. We all looked the same in that sea of black and
white uniforms, and I couldn't see her.

The bells struck nine and the older girls, the heads of each division, a black band around their left arm, made us parade in a single
line outside the cathedral. We had to goose-step on the cobblestones and shout the Fascist war cry, *"Eia, Eia, Alalà,"* three times.
We finally reached the far end of the square, where the stage had
been built and decorated with tricolor bunting and wooden columns shaped like wheat sheaves, the symbol of the Fascist Party.
The crowd parted like the Red Sea as we belted out the Fascist
hymn *Giovinezza,* marching two by two behind the oldest girl, who
carried the checkered flag.

On the stage I could see the party inspectors who'd come from
Milan for the occasion, together with the local council representatives and the archpriest in his ceremonial vestments. Around him
stood six halberdiers in a blue uniform and black bicorn hat adorned
with a large feather, which I thought funny and my father considered "pompous." Colombo should have been there too, but his seat
was empty.

Anxious, I waited for the moment I'd have to climb onstage alongside another girl with twin braids joined at the back of her neck, whose name I'd forgotten.

"Today, the Italian automotive industry will strike a decisive blow to conquer the top placements currently occupied by German constructors. And the Autodromo di Monza will be the theater of this much-awaited battle!" blared one of the party inspectors, and people clapped. By the time our turn came, the crowd was already thinning: the qualifying sessions began at 11 and the Autodromo was a good thirty-minute walk from the square.

I climbed onto the stage, my mouth dry. At a nod from the head of our division, I positioned myself under the microphone and began reciting the lines I'd learned by heart: "You shall pray and work for peace, but be prepared, in your heart, for war," I began, hands clasped behind my back as I tried to spot my mother in the crowd. "You can serve the motherland even by sweeping your house." And then I concluded in a clear, confident voice: "A nation's destiny rests on its women." A volley of half-hearted claps followed, the same you'd hear at a school play, and with the checkered flag finally blessed, the crowd dispersed. There was no trace of my mother and her red dress, but I didn't care anymore. I wanted to find Maddalena.

I finally spotted her, under the *Arengario* porticoes, with Ernesto and Luigia. Her uniform was all creased, the blouse had come untucked from her skirt, and an ice-cream stain stood out on her collar. She'd been chewing the cone from the bottom, so she was now having to lick the ice cream dripping from it. Luigia was sipping a lemonade, hands pressed against the glass bottle to absorb its coolness. She wore a men's shirt tucked into a calf-length skirt with a belt cinching her waist. Her hair was secured by a headband, revealing her small, round ears. Ernesto, by her side, was whispering something that made her laugh out loud. Maddalena saw me and waved.

"You didn't come to the parade," I said, joining them, "or the blessing of the flag."

She shrugged. "Couldn't be bothered. I was with Ernesto, who got me an ice cream. But I saw you, you know?"

"You did?"

"You were really good. Learned it all by heart."

"Thank you," I said, and I blushed thinking I must have looked beautiful up there, on a stage in Piazza Duomo, with all those important people, speaking with a microphone like those men on balconies in Rome.

"Do you believe any of that?" she asked, a grave look on her face.

"Any of what?"

"What you said on the stage. About women and the motherland."

I hesitated, worrying my lower lip. "I don't know. I hadn't thought about it."

"They're dangerous, you know."

"What's dangerous?"

"Words are," she answered. "They're dangerous if you don't think about what you're saying."

"They're just words . . ." I tried to joke, because her face was beginning to frighten me and I didn't want to argue.

But she kept staring at me. "They never are."

"Do you want to come with us?" asked Ernesto.

"We have refreshments!" Luigia lifted the wicker basket that rested in the crook of her arm.

"I've never seen a race up close," I replied. "My father thinks cars are too noisy."

"Does he? But that's the whole point!" said Ernesto, "We must remedy that!"

I'd learned to lie—I could come up with an excuse for my mother. And if she couldn't even be bothered to watch me while I was onstage, it meant that deep down, she didn't really care about me. On the way to the Autodromo, Ernesto told us about the recent remodeling of the racetrack and the speed the cars could attain on the straight stretch under the bleachers and around the bends. He told us about the big crash of 1933 that had cost the lives of not one but two drivers, Campari and Borzacchini, who had careened off the track. One had died on the spot, his rib cage crushed in the impact, and the other a few hours later, in the hospital. Was that the reason people flocked to car races? For the chance to witness a spectacular death, like the ancient Romans did with gladiators?

Ernesto's eyes twinkled. He was tugging at Luigia's hand, urging her on, not wanting to miss a single minute, not even the qualifying sessions. He was like a child in a candy store. Luigia laughed, and it occurred to me that maybe that was all it took to be happy: holding hands, sharing in the happiness of someone you loved.

Rows of cars covered by large white sheets to protect them from the scorching sun were parked on the lawn by the track. Spectators crowded the bleachers, others were pressed flush against the fences around the car park. The place smelled of squashed grass, sweaty jackets, and homemade sandwiches. We picked our way across the dry lawn, skirting around families on picnic blankets and clusters of supporters huddled against the hay barriers that separated them from the track. We jumped up when we passed the cameras, hoping to make it into the shot. Maybe the next time I went to the movie theater, I'd be able to point at the screen and say, "That's me, I was there!"

Luigia walked holding a magazine over her head to shield her eyes from the sun, while Ernesto pointed out where to step so her heels wouldn't sink in the lawn. He led us on, repeating, "Excuse us," as we inched through the crowd to find the best spots and watch the start of the race. The single-seaters paraded on the race-track, escorted by the mechanics in their white overalls. They were long and shiny like torpedoes and looked like tin toys. Nuvolari's Alfa Romeo was number 20. All hopes were on him to beat the Germans.

Before the race could begin, the cars had to complete the qualifying sessions to determine the starting positions. It was hot, and Maddalena and I were restless, impatient to start eating, but Ernesto insisted we had to wait until the race had started, as tradition dictated. Excitement quickly gave way to boredom. We lay on the grass counting the orange bubbles that popped behind our shuttered eyelids while Luigia secretly handed us lard sandwiches wrapped in greasy paper.

"It's time." Ernesto shook us.

The engines revved louder and the spectators pointed at the track: the race was about to begin. After the Italian flag was ceremonially raised over the wheat-sheaf-shaped tower and saluted by a sea of raised arms, the authorities began examining the cars that had taken their place at the start line, while the carabinieri in their bicorn hats monitored the crowds. The atmosphere was electric, the head-splitting roar of the engines vibrating all the way up my nose. Maddalena and I covered our ears, laughing. And then the single-seaters were off to the enthusiastic cries of the crowd, gone in the blink of an eye. The drivers pushed the cars so hard, as if they weren't afraid to die.

I really couldn't see what all the excitement was about: the noise of the engines would rise then fall, cars darting away like flies, and from where we were seated it was impossible to understand how the race was progressing.

"Look at them go!" shouted Ernesto, then promised Luigia that with his next raise he'd set aside enough money to buy a convertible and he'd drive her to the beach in it, maybe all the way to Genoa or Sanremo.

"Is there room for us too?" said a familiar voice. Donatella wore a tight dress that hugged her bosom, pearl earrings, a warm coral hue on her lips, and Tiziano Colombo's arm draped around hers. He dipped his head in greeting.

He was in his uniform: plus fours, black shirt, white gaiters, and a neckerchief embroidered with a wheat sheaf interlaced with the letter *M* over the word *vincere*—"to be victorious." Tiziano was sleek and fair, smooth cheeks ever so slightly damp, perhaps with cologne, a thick coat of pomade on his hair. "Forgive the intrusion," he pleaded. "She insisted on saying hello."

"No problem at all," replied Luigia. "The more the merrier!" She scooted closer to Ernesto so Donatella and Tiziano could sit.

He introduced himself, carefully enunciating his name: "Tiziano Colombo" he announced to the group. "Pleased to meet you all."

Then his gaze landed on me and lingered for a long time, as if to examine me. Embarrassed, I crossed my arms over my chest, where my blouse stretched uncomfortably.

"Mr. Strada's daughter," he said finally, smiling. "My father told me about you, you know?" His thumb stroked the golden badge as he continued, "He said you were still a little girl, but you look all grown up to me."

I couldn't answer. My mouth felt thick with cotton wool.

They talked about the heat and the cars, about the mosquitoes that kept everyone awake at night, and the Germans who were rubbish drivers. Then Luigia took out the remaining sandwiches— cheese and salami—and the lemonades. It didn't take long for the men to start discussing the war.

"Nah, it won't happen, trust me," Ernesto was saying, "It's been almost a year since they signed the agreement, hasn't it? Everyone's forgotten about that mess at the Walwal oasis."

That bizarre name sounded like some animal noise to me. I'd heard it once from my father, months before, and quickly forgot it.

Something to do with a clash between Italy and Ethiopia over a strip of land rich in groundwater: that was all I knew.

"An affront that cannot go unpunished much longer. What about our pride as a nation?" Tiziano parried.

"We could use some of that pride at home," laughed Ernesto. "We've enough problems here, no need to go looking for trouble in the sands of Africa."

"If it did come to war, would you go, Merlini?" Tiziano challenged him.

"There won't be any wars," Luigia butted in, on edge, taking Ernesto's hand in hers.

He was twenty and could be drafted into the national service, but in case that happened, he was hoping to delay his departure with the excuse of the wedding.

"If I could, I'd go in a heartbeat," Tiziano continued, eyes glinting. A waft of his cologne reached us.

"Well, you couldn't even if you wanted to," Donatella said, tugging at his arm, "And enough of this nonsense, it'll spoil our Sunday. And it'll keep me awake at night!"

Tiziano smiled. "My apologies, ladies. We didn't mean to upset you. The sandwiches are delicious, thank you," he added, with a nod to Luigia.

"Why can't you?" the Cursed One cut in all of a sudden. I turned to face her, as did all the others. She had that grave look on her face, the look that signaled things were about to get serious. "If you're so keen to fight, why don't you go?"

"Oh, Maddalena, enough of this. No one's declared war on anyone." Donatella leaned forward to grab a lemonade.

"Alas, my heart is no match for my courage," Tiziano replied, looking resigned.

"And what's that supposed to mean?" Maddalena insisted.

"Congenital heart condition," Tiziano clarified, spitting out those words as if they caused him pain. "My heart was born wrong. The doctors hear a strong murmur in between heartbeats," he continued, his eyes now sad, almost desperate. "Even if I tried to enlist, they'd turn me away. Unfit. And that's the sad truth."

"Oh, come on! Lucky is what you are. You can be safe, at home," said Donatella, biting off a chunk of her sandwich. "Why are you men so obsessed with war?"

"For the motherland," Tiziano replied at once.

"The motherland won't feed ya or clothe ya or put a roof over yer head!" Donatella mocked him, her language getting coarser despite her lipstick and pearls. Men and all their talk of motherland and war—it was all hot air, there was no substance to it.

"Abyssinia's riches could keep our whole country for a century!" Tiziano bit back, seemingly offended by the crude common sense that made a mockery of his lofty statements.

Donatella rolled her eyes, bored. Luigia stared anxiously at Ernesto.

"Why is war such a beautiful thing to you?" Maddalena, again.

"Right, that's enough now," Luigia blurted out, trying to inject some gaiety into her brittle voice. "We're all here to have a good time, and I won't have any more talk of this rotten war!"

We were all quiet, nothing but the midday heat and the hum of chirping insects around us. The Cursed One sought my eyes, immediately looking away when she found them.

"Come, we can't miss the end of the race!" Ernesto said, rising to his feet.

Luigia followed him, shaking, as if war had broken out there and then. Donatella stood too, wobbling on her heels. She ran a finger across her lips: "Lipstick's all smudged . . ."

"I told you you don't need makeup to look beautiful" Tiziano consoled her. "It makes no difference at all." And he led her toward the track, a hand resting on her lower back.

The cars roared in with an unholy racket, all hurtling across the finish line at the same time, or so it seemed to me. People were shouting, waving their hats: "Who came first? Did anyone see the number? The flag? Was it black and yellow or green and red?"

The winner was Hans Stuck, a German. Nuvolari came second, although he'd clocked the fastest lap. "Germans. Never liked them," commented Ernesto.

The loudspeakers were blaring out Germany's national hymn, the language so harsh and consonant-heavy that I could only imagine mean things being said in it. Tazio Nuvolari, small and lean, stood on a lower block on the podium, waving at the crowd, an Italian flag draped over his shoulders. His face was caked in soot except for the eyes, where the goggles had left a clean, white mask. Hans Stuck was tall and blond, with a mousy face.

Luigia's head came to rest on Ernesto's shoulder: "What will happen if they declare war for real? What are we going to do?"

"God won't allow it," replied Ernesto, planting a kiss on her hair.

After the race, Maddalena and I headed to the river, talking about war and love on our way back to the town center. She didn't believe in either. She liked Luigia, but her mother didn't because the girl had no dowry and her father was a communist. Tiziano, however, she couldn't stomach because of his cruel smile and the way he always took care not to soil his uniform—the uniform he wore even when he didn't need to, with a pride that disgusted her: "It's a mask," Maddalena was saying. "And if you're always wearing a mask, it means you've got something to hide." Her mother liked Tiziano because he was from a powerful family and his father had once shaken

Mussolini's hand, or so he said. But above all, Mrs. Merlini liked Tiziano because he was rich, and every Saturday he took Donatella out for a drive to the lakes in his father's black Balilla, and they'd go on the steamer and eat in a restaurant. These were things she'd never even dreamed of for herself, but for her daughter, she wanted a big fancy wedding, and holidays in a spa town to "take the waters" as she'd heard rich people say, and chubby, clean-faced grandchildren. Maddalena thought Tiziano was a *bauscia*, a braggart, who put on airs but would never come up to scratch.

"I like him," I said. "He's elegant, polite. He speaks well too, uses difficult words. And I like his manners."

"And what does he speak about?" she blurted out. "War! War's just a game to him, like a child playing with his toy soldiers."

"Are you afraid of him?"

"Of that loudmouth?"

"You don't fancy him, by any chance? I think he's rather handsome," I teased.

"I'm not afraid of anything," she hissed. "And I don't fancy anyone. Let alone someone like *him*." She picked up the pace.

When we reached Leoni bridge I realized we were running and I was out of breath. The four lions on the columns stared at us, hostile, their paws crossed, like schoolteachers waiting to scold us.

The river was so full you couldn't see the rocks at the bottom. Filippo and Matteo were waiting for us on the shore, one in his Balilla uniform, socks still on, the other in his usual stained vest, barefoot already.

"Took your time!" Matteo said as the Cursed One and I slid down the crumbled section of the embankment, torn ivy leaves and snapped branches marking the spot we'd crossed countless times. Maddalena held out her arm to help me down while I kept one hand on my skirt to stop it riding up.

"We thought you weren't coming," Filippo began. "And it's hot as hell down here."

The Cursed One marched down to the shore, shoes clacking on the pebbles. "Do you know what we're going to do now? We're going in."

"In the water? Dressed like this?"

"No, not like this," she replied, laughing. "We're going to take our clothes off."

"What do you mean?" I asked.

"We'll be in our vests and panties. It'll be like going to the beach!"

"What do you know about the beach? You've never been," teased Matteo.

"And you have?" Maddalena snapped. "And anyway what do we care? We'll make our own beach here—just for us, which is even better. Come on!" And she whipped her blouse off, dropping it on the pebbles. Then she toed off her shoes and kicked them away. "What are you waiting for?" she called out as her skirt came off too. She was in her panties now, and a white vest too big for her lean shoulders. Her spine jutted out under the fair skin of her back, straight and ridged. She was so beautiful.

The Cursed One took a run-up and dove into the Lambro, then reemerged, panting, her mouth open: "Water's cold!" she shouted. "Bunch of scaredy-cats! C'mon, jump in!"

Matteo went first—he didn't even take off his vest and shorts. As soon as he got to the water he let out a piercing cry, like an animal noise. He and Maddalena pushed each other under, laughing and swallowing water and coughing as they stood back up. Filippo took off his uniform almost in a rage. He dove in and shot back out, shaking and hugging his chest, breath coming in little uneven spurts, mouth wide open: "It's *cold!*" he hissed through his teeth. Matteo was on him at once, kicking up water with his feet.

And then I slipped out of my blouse and skirt. It felt like shedding an old unwanted dress, dirty and too tight. I took a run-up. After a summer of walking barefoot, the soles of my feet had turned to leather—I didn't even feel the stones. I dove in, eyes shut, and the icy water ripped my breath to shreds.

"Water's too cold, I'm telling you!" said Filippo, flailing as he tried to escape to the shore.

"Quit whining like a little girl!" Matteo growled as he grabbed one of his legs. Filippo tried to wrench it free and they started fighting, shouting and pulling each other's hair. The Cursed One barged in between them, pushing them both back into the Lambro, and the fight turned into a chaotic scuffle back and forth from the shore, as they tried to push each other into the water.

"Are you just gonna stand there and watch?" Maddalena asked.

I crossed myself and dove into the tussle.

And as I clashed and punched, grazing my knees on the murky riverbed, toes sinking in the same black mud that caked my hair, I was made flesh. I was skin and blood, bones and bruises. And sharp edges, and cries. I was alive. For the first time in my life, with the Cursed Ones, I could say "I'm here" and feel all the weight of that statement.

I grabbed one of Maddalena's arms and thrust a foot behind her knees like I'd seen her do when she fought with the boys on the shore. She shrieked and toppled over backward into the water, black hair sticking to her forehead like seaweed when she came back up.

She stood, laughing. "Now you've done it!" she said, grabbing my waist and throwing me off balance. I didn't even have time to catch my breath, and then everything was water. I swallowed that murky iciness, kicking madly, thinking I was going to die. It was Maddalena who hauled me out, tugging at my wrist. I coughed violently, a hand pressed to my chest, then burst out laughing. The panic washed off her face and she hugged me. It felt good, her skin on mine.

The shadows cast by the bridge and the buildings along the

embankment now stretched across the whole riverbed. Still clinging to the Cursed One, I realized I was shaking.

"C'mon, let's get in the sun, or we'll never dry off," she said.
Her fingers, interlaced in mine, sparked a sudden rush of heat that
pooled at the base of my neck.

We lay down in the only remaining slice of light on the riverbank,
eyes closed, pebbles digging into our backs, catching our breath as
rivulets of water trailed off our temples and down the edges of our
motionless bodies.

"I want to stay like this forever," I said, my skin slowly warming.

"You mean wet and shaking?" she teased, laughing.

"I mean with you."

I heard the crunch of shingle and I knew she was moving. When
her shadow blocked out the sun I opened my eyes and saw her, lying
on one side, chin resting in her hand. "I'm coming to school next
month."

"Really?"

"Ernesto said I could," she nodded. "He wants me to keep study-
ing. He'll take care of everything, but I'm not allowed to fail."

"You just have to apply yourself."

"That's not the problem—I can make an effort. But the rest . . .
you'll have to teach me."

"What can I teach *you*? I know nothing."

"You know how to be good," she retorted. "You can teach me to
behave."

She lay back down and spread out her arms and legs, as if to
make a snow angel.

That's when I felt a sudden tug in my belly, excruciating pain, as
if someone was treading on me. The ache disappeared only to return
stronger when I drew my next breath. I sat up. There was something
dark stuck to my thigh, trickling down in a thin black line. I thought

it must be seaweed, some slimy twig from the riverbed, and I reached down to peel it off. As I touched it, however, I saw that my fingers had gone red, glistening with blood. I shot up, hobbling, trying to find my balance as my nostrils filled with the dank, unpleasant smell I remembered from when Maddalena and I had sat on "cat island" comparing scratches.

I stood still as fat drops slid down my calves and pooled on the pebbles, dark as the copper coins Carla stacked up on the kitchen table before heading out to buy bread.

"I'm dying!" I cried.

"What's going on?" shouted Matteo, still in the water.

"Is that . . . blood?" asked Filippo.

"Shut up," cut in the Cursed One.

I cupped my hands between my legs to try and stem the bleeding. I was about to be turned inside out like a rag doll. My guts would spill and that's how I was going to die, grungy and hollowed out on the banks of the Lambro. "I'm dying!"

Then I heard Maddalena's voice whispering in my ear: "You mustn't be afraid."

I grasped her sodden vest as I felt my legs give in, and I had to hold on to her to steady myself. Pain washed over me in waves, another scorching tug stealing the air from my lungs. Breathing was a deliberate effort, a chore.

Maddalena raked her fingers through my hair, now stiff with mud. "Breathe." Her words ran through me, soothing like water. "It'll go away."

A chilling sense of calm washed down my spine, like a finger brushing every notch of my vertebrae. The shivers stopped, as did the pain.

"Everything's all right," said Maddalena, "It's normal. I told you we mustn't be afraid of blood."

"How did you know?"

"Donatella gets it every month. Her belly and back hurt for a few days, then it goes away."

"Every m-month?" I stammered. "But . . . it can't be. This will kill me."

"I told you you're not dying," she shot back, gravely. She gripped my shoulders and forced me to look at her. "All women get this. It's what happens when you grow up."

"Do *you* get it?"

"Not yet."

"Why do only women get it?"

She shrugged. "I don't know. I think it's the way we're made, and that's that."

She stretched her arms, peeling me away from her, and looked me up and down like my mother did before we left the house. She led me to the shore, then back into the water.

Breathing was easy again, and I let Maddalena help me wash the blood away. She made me remove my panties, now soiled, then rubbed my thighs.

"I'm sorry," I said.

"You're all right."

"About your vest, I mean." I pointed at a red smear I'd left on her side.

"What do I care about that?" she replied.

Tears pricked at my eyelashes.

"Don't you cry now!"

"I'm not crying," I replied, wiping my face with the palm of my hand. "Crying is for idiots."

She smiled. "You've been paying attention."

Matteo and Filippo crouched on the riverbed, water lapping at their shoulders, and watched us.

"What's the matter with you?" asked Matteo, smoothing a dripping lock of hair off his forehead.

"Nothing's the matter."

Filippo bent forward, dipped his head in the water and started blowing bubbles from his nose: "So why is there blood?"

"When we get hurt we don't make such a fuss," Matteo added. "Let me have a look."

"That's none of your business!" the Cursed One snapped. "What do you know about this? And stop staring!"

We waded out and made for the shore, then put our clothes back on, our skin still wet. Maddalena had skipped a button on her blouse and her black skirt was all askew, the fabric clinging to her thighs. She reached underneath it and peeled off her panties, cocking one leg, then the other. "Here," she said. "Yours are soiled."

"But what about you?"

She shrugged. "It doesn't matter."

I took the panties she handed me, still wet, and quickly slid them on. They were cold and stuck to my skin. I straightened, bunching mine in my hand. "You know . . . the things they say about you?"

She stopped fussing with her blouse and raised her head. "What about it?"

"They're not true," I told her. "It's not true that you bring bad luck, or that story about the devil's mark. It's not true that bad things will happen to me when I'm with you."

She kept staring at me without saying a word, a grave look on her face.

"With you, I feel safe."

Part II

Today's
SINS,
Tomorrow's
BLOOD

10.

*T*he black Balilla was parked outside my house, on the opposite side of the street, near the barber shop and the posters advertising Cinzano vermouth. Colombo was in the driver's seat, face hidden by his hat. Next to him, in her red dress, sat my mother.

I froze, unable to look away. They were close, talking animatedly, and my mother laughed, unguarded, her mouth wide open, like I'd never seen her do at home. The windshield blocked all sound, and it was like watching a puppet show. My mother must have spotted me, because she suddenly collected herself, nodded at Colombo, and opened the door, tidying her hair and smoothing her skirt as she stepped out of the car. Then she walked up to me, heels clacking on the road. "It is not polite to stare, Francesca." She paused, licking her lips. "Mr. Colombo was kind enough to drive me home. Now, be a good girl and say hello."

Colombo nodded in greeting, tipping his hat. My mother waved at him, giggling like a schoolgirl, then turned to face me. Only then did she appear to actually see me. "Just what did you do to your uniform?" she questioned me, grimacing.

I didn't answer. Soiled panties bunched in one hand, creased gloves in the other, I darted through the gate and up the stairs as my mother called after me from the street. As soon as I was through the door, Carla—who knew me from the way my shoes clacked on the tiles—said hello from the kitchen.

My father looked up from behind his newspaper: "I got you the children's supplement." Then he saw me. "What happened to you? Did you fall into the river?"

My face burned with shame at being seen like that by him. I ran to the bathroom and immediately began washing the blood-soaked panties, fearing I'd be scolded.

"What exactly is the matter with your daughter?" my mother asked, on edge.

"Weren't you together?" my father replied. "Where did you leave her?"

I rubbed the soap bar harder, its sharp edges digging into the palms of my hands as the water ran pink and the sickeningly sweet smells of blood and lavender rose to my nostrils.

"She must have been running around with those ragamuffins again," my mother was saying. "Mrs. Mauri saw her with the Cursed One."

"Who? The Merlini girl?"

"I don't like that girl. I knew she'd lead her astray."

"You know nothing!" I shouted from the bathroom, biting back my tears.

Unexpected silence. My mother was the first to speak, demanding my father discipline me for my impertinence. He refused, and when she insisted, he said that was enough. He yelled it.

I froze, petrified, my fingers gripping the edge of the sink. My father never yelled.

Suddenly the bathroom door was flung open, revealing a flash of red—my mother's dress. We stared at each other for a long time, me, standing by the sink, legs bare, arms lathered in soap, she, on the threshold, eyes round with surprise. "I see," she said softly. She didn't elaborate, save for a "You're a woman now," delivered in an impersonal tone.

For a moment, she seemed not to recognize me, as if I were some threatening creature she had tried and failed to tame. Opening the bathroom cabinet, she laid out long strips of fabric on the bath, then a bottle marked "Sanadon." "These are for the blood," she said, pointing at the cloths. "And that's for the pain. See that you clean up after yourself. And next time, remember to just say, 'I'm indisposed.' Anything else is just unseemly."

Then the door closed behind her. "It's nothing. Female problems." I heard her curt reply to my father's inquiries from the living room. I just stood there, stupefied, until Carla broke me out of my trance with a knock on the door.

"May I?" she ventured, coming in with a friendly smile. She took a long breath, gathered the supplies my mother had left on the bath, and kneeled on the floor. "Here's how you do it."

The pain stopped within a week, as did the blood. My body, however, seemed to grow more alien by the day, which I struggled to come to terms with. For the first time, I was aware of people's eyes on me, especially male eyes. I'd go down to the Lambro with the Cursed Ones in a tattered dress, or accompany my mother on her errands looking all prim and proper, and always, always, I'd feel people's gaze on me, hear their whispered comments.

"It's because you're pretty," my mother reassured me, noticing my distress. But I didn't feel pretty. Being noticed by men made me feel guilty. Once home, I'd lock myself up in the bathroom and study my reflection in the mirror, naked, ashamed of the acne that disfigured my cheeks and forehead and chin, ashamed of the swelling, dilating flesh underneath my nipples. I mourned my childhood.

Toward the end of September, all the talk outside the newsagents and the church was of "Italian Abyssinia," "the sands of victory," and "death to the negus." One day, my father came home with a bottle of sparkling wine—an expensive one—and announced that celebrations were in order. He dug out a record of popular opera arias and asked Carla to set the table and make saffron risotto, his favorite.

I hadn't seen him that happy in a long time. He sang, in his booming, off-key voice: *"E a te, mia dolce Aida, tornar di lauri cinto. Dirti: per te ho pugnato, per te ho vinto!"* When Carla offered to help him uncork the wine, he seemed offended, insisting he'd take care of it himself. There were no sausages, but the risotto was still delicious, and the bread, fresh from the bakery, crackled under my fingers, warm and fragrant.

"What are we celebrating?" asked my mother, who wasn't used to drinking, her cheeks already ruddy.

"The contract for the troops' hats," Dad replied, "is officially ours."

My mother lifted her glass for Carla to refill. "Colombo kept his word," she commented, pride flashing in her eyes.

"All thanks to our top-quality felt!" My father took a sip and smacked his lips, then added, "And if this blessed war actually breaks out, you'll see how the orders will shoot up!"

I didn't want war, but I was glad to see my father so happy. Luckily, the embarrassment I'd caused when the Colombos had come for lunch hadn't sunk his deal. And he would still love me.

I mopped up what was left of the risotto with a chunk of bread. In those days, I was ravenous, insatiable. "Wiped the plate clean!" teased my father as the bread moistened.

My mother glared at us. "That's not at all proper!"

"Oh, leave her be, she's a growing girl!" my father laughed. "And a pretty girl at that, our Francesca. A few years and there'll be a queue at the door, I'm telling you. We'll have to fend suitors off with clubs!"

I wrapped my arms around my stomach, where it strained against the belt, and kept chewing. Carla cleared the table without a word, then paused at the kitchen door and crossed herself. She was scared. She believed it was only ever honest people who died in wars, while the powers that be sent them away like lambs to the slaughter without a care in the world.

"I can feel it in my bones," my father reprised, wiping his mouth with his napkin, "from now on, it'll all work out for the best."

11.

The declaration of war came on the evening of October 2.

It was cold as hell, and the *scighera*, the autumn fog, was thick as butter. Piazza Trento was heaving, the shrouded crowd only discernible from the muffled thrum of expectation. A scratchy hiss emanated from the loudspeakers as the authorities waited on the town hall balcony, cocooned in their uniforms, backs ramrod straight and hands on their hips. Flashes of the national flag and bunting emerged from the mist only to disappear again, together with the brass trumpet on the monument to the fallen.

"Do they really think this is something to celebrate?" Maddalena said, her gaze on the ground.

Suddenly the loudspeakers crackled, and Mussolini's voice seemed to materialize out of nothing, thundering and proud. He paused to breathe far too often, however, which reminded me of the fish opening and closing their mouths, their slimy eyes bulging out when Maddalena caught them and squeezed them in her fingers.

Mussolini spoke with passion about the men and women who had gathered in town squares all over Italy: "Their presence must prove, and indeed proves to the world, that Italy and Fascism are but one perfect, absolute, unalterable identity. Only those whose brains are addled by crass ignorance, ignorance of this Italy and its people in 1935, the thirteenth year of the Fascist era, could believe that not to be the case. For months now the wheel of destiny—propelled by our calm determination—has been spinning toward its inevitable destination, and spinning ever faster now, unstoppable now!"

The crowd burst into loud cheers and chants, a single, monstrous being, shapeless, headless, swallowing us. The loudspeakers blared out speeches and songs all evening, and everywhere in town people seemed consumed by an unusual feeling of euphoria, as if only now, in that war cry, they'd finally found their purpose. As if a few words from a man they'd only seen in portraits in the town hall or at the movie theater, speaking from a balcony in a faraway city they only knew from postcards or book illustrations, had sufficed to remind them they were but one people, one country, under one leader and one God.

They sang *"Faccetta Nera,"* a popular song about a beautiful Ethiopian slave rescued by Italian troops, and waved flags with such fervor that the mist briefly cleared in their wake. I felt that ancient, animal energy coursing through me like thunder. I still couldn't fathom how news of an impending conflict could be met with such joy, same as, say, a holiday would, yet I couldn't help but be swept away by that unrestrained power. Being part of something felt wonderful, even something so chaotic, reckless, dangerous.

Three days after Italy declared war against Ethiopia, Ernesto received his official summons. He turned up at the local draft center in a clean shirt and tie and requested to delay his departure until after the wedding, in the spring. No one listened. All Italian men had to contribute to the cause, and little did children, wives, or ailing parents matter—they'd simply be awaiting the return of their beloved, in the name of the motherland. Sacrifices were being demanded of us all for "the greater good," although it was unclear to me what this greater good consisted of.

Donatella had offered to ask Tiziano if his father could be per-
suaded to intercede on Ernesto's behalf: "A man in his position, he'll
find a way, for sure."

Ernesto gritted his teeth: "And what for? So I can strut around
town blabbering about war and cursing my incurable heart condition? No, I'd rather go to Abyssinia—at least I'll come back with a
clear conscience. With pride. Free. I don't want anything to do with
these Fascists!"

Donatella was in tears, saying he didn't know what he was talking
about. "And what am I to do with your pride, huh?" begged Luigia.
"Better Fascist here than free in Africa. If not dead in Africa!"

Eyes bulging out in rage, Ernesto banged his hands on the table
and insisted nothing in the world would make him give up on his
principles. In his life, he'd only ever promised to honor the Lord and
Luigia, and he wanted to pledge himself to her again, and forever,
before a priest, rice stuck in his collar and all. He'd saved enough
for his family not to go without while he was away, he said. Then,
when he saw Luigia shaking and exhaling a long breath, he kissed
her forehead and said, "I'll be back in no time, you'll see."

Luigia removed her fogged-up glasses, pressing her face to his
chest, and tried for a smile. "And with you gone, how are we ever
going to finish the dress?"

On October 6 we sat at the dinner table in complete silence, listening to the radio as the soup cooled in our bowls. A stern but calm
voice announced that the Italian troops had conquered Adwa. The
first victory, a mere three days since the start of the conflict. Carla
was in the kitchen, praying to the Lord for the war to end soon. Her
younger brother, who was forever repeating Mussolini's motto, "The
more the enemies, the greater the honor," had enlisted.

"The journey toward world expansion has begun," the radio was saying. "Our mission as a great colonial nation starts from Adwa, reconquered and reclaimed for Christianity."

War wasn't that complicated a game after all. Ernesto would be back soon and there would be even more cause for celebration at the wedding. Come spring, there would be flowers in the bride's tresses, and for once Maddalena's hair would be tidy and her shoes polished. I'd buy a new dress, a grown-up dress cinched at the waist, hem grazing my ankles. Maddalena would laugh and we'd dance, my toes balanced on hers.

12.

*E*rnesto was to leave on the morning of Monday the 14th, which was also the first day of school. He would be joining a battalion for a few weeks of training and then be deployed to Africa. Luigia had been praying for Ernesto to be assigned to a regiment in Italy, Verona perhaps, or Florence, but her prayers hadn't been answered. Heaven, I figured, must be not unlike the local draft center, where nobody would give a little seamstress the time of day.

Maddalena wanted to skip school and walk Ernesto to the army truck. She wanted to keep saying goodbye until he'd disappear down the road, her throat hoarse from shouting. But he'd made her promise she wouldn't miss a single day of school and that she'd always be on her best behavior.

"I want to see top grades on all subjects." He'd planted a kiss on her cheek, right on that blemish people thought was the mark of the devil. "Keep the faith."

The Sunday before Ernesto's departure, the Merlinis hosted a farewell lunch. Maddalena's mother served a glistening, piping-hot boiled salami sausage, and *castagnaccio* cake with pine nuts and raisins. I'd been invited too. "You're practically family," Ernesto had said.

Luigia, eyes swollen with tears, wouldn't stop biting her lip, while

Donatella sat alone by the window, smoking a cigarette she'd extracted from a silver case—a gift from Tiziano Colombo. For days she'd been arguing with Ernesto because he wouldn't let her help him, and now that there was no escaping war, she resented him. "He and his blasted pride," she said. "For all the good it'll do him!"

The atmosphere was gloomy despite Ernesto's attempts to lighten the mood. Although it was cold, the window had been left open so we could hear the music float in from the floor above. When the radio played *"Faccetta Nera,"* Ernesto shut the glass panes and began rolling a cigarette, moistening the paper on his lips, without saying a word. Smoke filled the kitchen as his face darkened. Maddalena's mother sat at the head of the table, scratched her fork on the empty plate, and began: "If Mussolini knew about these injustices, he wouldn't allow it. We should let him know how we struggle, us poor people. We could write a letter . . ."

Luigia's eyes sought Ernesto as a bitter laugh escaped him. "And what does he care?"

"Divine providence saved him from those assassination attempts! That shows the saints are protecting him . . ." his mother insisted.

"All that shows is that he's like a fly, that one!" Ernesto slammed his hand on the table, sending flecks of tobacco swirling in the air. "Hard to kill. You've got to really put your heart into it. Try again and again until it's done."

Luigia put the kettle on for the barley coffee. Maddalena, meanwhile, took me to the bedroom she shared with her siblings. I spied a crucifix and an icon of Saint Francis nailed to the wall above Ernesto's bed, next to newspaper clippings with photos of Nuvolari and Learco Guerra, who had won the Giro d'Italia the previous year. On Donatella's bedside table, a postcard with Vittorio De Sica in a scene from *What Scoundrels Men Are!,* a little tub of face powder, and a popular crime novel.

Maddalena's side was bare, except for the gleaming pebbles she gathered by the river. The room was just large enough for the beds, allowing no privacy. She gestured me to sit on her bed, the lumpy mattress sagging under my weight, then told me she couldn't sleep at night. She'd count the cracks on the ceiling, she said, then throw off the blanket and try to pray. But she couldn't. "You have to teach me. I just can't make it work . . ."

"It's not something you can teach . . ."

"Of course it is," she insisted. "Do I have to kneel like this? And then what? Do I have to speak all proper to the Virgin Mary? Say 'please' and 'thank you'?"

"Why do you want to pray all of a sudden?"

"I just want him back safe," she said, eyes so dark. "And I'll never ask for anything else in my life."

I'd never seen her so low. Her stubbornness, her rage couldn't help her now. But her eyes were dry, and fierce as ever when I kneeled on the floor next to her, elbows perched on the bed, forehead resting on my clasped hands. Together we recited the Hail Mary and Our Father, Maddalena trailing behind because she couldn't remember the words well. With her by my side, faith seemed to regain meaning, a human dimension, far from churches and incense. With Maddalena, I secretly began to believe in God again.

When it was time to go home, Ernesto came to say goodbye. "I'm glad Maddalena found you," he said, tapping an unlit cigarette on the palm of his hand, his shoulders stiff. His movements had the same rawness as his sister's, the same vulnerability too, which he hid behind a face that would have sent the devil himself running.

"People call her vicious names," he continued, slotting the cigarette between his lips. "She wears them like an armor, she's proud of them now. Strong girl. Doesn't care what people say. These days, it's the only thing that matters."

"She's not afraid of anything," I said, trying to tip my chin up like she did.

"That's not always a good thing." He lit the cigarette, inhaled. "Promise me you'll be by her side."

I felt important, entrusted with a sacred task, the heroine of one of those cloak-and-dagger novels where characters used difficult words and gave their lives for each other.

"I promise."

The following day I informed my mother I didn't want Carla to walk me to school anymore now that I was a woman. I put my coat on, grabbed the schoolbag packed with brand-new notebooks, and left the house by myself, the crisp morning air slapping my face and mussing my hair. Maddalena was waiting for me at the fountain outside Palazzo Frette, down by Piazza Mazzini.

"It'll be boring for you," I said as we walked side by side on the pavement. "You'll have to listen to the same things you heard last year."

Maddalena was running a stick along the iron railings. "It's different now. You weren't here last year. And I promised I'd behave."

Her face was clean, hair tucked neatly behind her ears, socks gleaming white. "A year goes by so quickly, you'll see." She reached for my hand and rubbed her thumb over my cracked knuckles. "Come on, we'll be late."

I was happy and scared on my first day at such a prestigious school. It made me feel like a grown-up. I had studied hard for the entrance examination in my last year of primary school, and the thought that I might not pass had given me terrible nightmares. School, with its rules, its timetables and grades, seemed to give me purpose, a target to achieve. There was a clear path I could understand, a mission—same as in novels.

We arrived, panting, still holding hands. There were separate entrances—boys to one side, girls to the other—and separate classes too, as if God himself had erected a barrier between man and woman that would fall only through marriage. I'd have felt lost but for Maddalena's hand clasped in mine, guiding me through the gate adorned with tricolor bunting, then across the yard and up the staircase. We passed a large portrait of Rosa Maltoni, Mussolini's mother and a former schoolteacher, looking meek and compliant. Garlands and roses lay on the floor under the portrait as if on an altar.

Our classroom was on the second floor. Large windows flooded the space with light, and portraits of the king, queen, and duce hung on the far wall next to a crucifix. The blackboard smelled of soap, and brand-new erasers had been neatly stacked on a wooden shelf.

Maddalena took me to a desk at the back: from there, you could look out the window and let your mind wander.

"I worked at this all of last year," she said proudly, pointing at a finger-wide hole piercing the desktop from side to side.

"Shall we sit here?"

"No. This year we're sitting at the front."

The other girls cast curious glances as we crossed the room, hand in hand, headed for the front-row desks where nobody dared sit. Hair braided tightly or tied up in ribbons, knees smooth as kneaded bread dough, our classmates sat up straight, backs stiff, ankles crossed. Although she was a year older, the Cursed One was a good inch shorter than everyone else, the ribbon on her uniform deliberately undone, cuts and bruises on display.

Our Italian and Latin teacher walked in, and we rose to greet her. After taking attendance, she introduced herself with a few curt sentences. She had no time for slackers, she announced, and would not tolerate complaints. With her permission, we took our places in a buzz of muted mutterings. The twin desks were covered in graffiti carved by generations of pocketknives.

I was panting, already fearing I wouldn't be good enough, but Maddalena's hand came to rest on my thigh under the desk, and the familiar, wholesome smell of her skin calmed me. "I'm here," she said. And that was enough.

Maddalena was doing her best, but it was clear that school was not for her.

The ribbon on her uniform bothered her, as did asking for permission to use the restroom or saying, "Excuse me, Miss." Most of all, she hated the morning ritual of the Fascist salute: we had to stand ramrod straight next to our desks, right arm stretched forward, fingers pointing at Mussolini's portrait, heels clacking as we prayed to the Lord to protect "the duce, the royal family, and our beloved motherland." The other girls cast sidelong glances at her shoes, her knees, the bad haircut, the gleaming mark on her temple. During recess they'd lean against the radiators with their white-bread sandwiches and laugh at her black bread, and when she said, "Whatcha looking at?" they'd scuttle away, tail tucked between their legs.

As for me, I was beginning to enjoy school, although I was already struggling with Latin. I loved the sound of the ancient language, however, and I was captivated by all the stories of gods and heroes, battles and clever schemes, and undying love. If Monza were to burn like Troy, I'd carry Maddalena away on my shoulders and we'd run without ever looking back. Then we'd found our own country and reign over it as queens.

I'd always been described as a "quiet, well-mannered" girl. That wasn't enough anymore. I wanted them to say my name and then, in the same breath, "She's the smartest." I liked earning the tricolor rosettes, being told I'd done a good job. The most important lessons, however, remained Maddalena's: how to skim pebbles on the river, why boys chased girls, how babies swelled their mothers' bellies before they were born. The things Maddalena taught me were at once simple and mysterious, but shrouded in shame and reticence by the grown-ups—forbidden, clandestine, and therefore infinitely more interesting.

I realized compliments meant more if they came from her. I liked that she admired me if I helped her with a complicated math exercise or explained the difference between direct and indirect objects in a sentence. "You just get them straightaway, these things, don't you?" she'd say, turning her attention back to her dog-eared notebook covered in ink splotches. She worked hard for her brother, to whom she wrote once a week—and for that, she came to me. Finally, since the start of our friendship, I realized I could give something back. Till then, I'd always felt dispensable before.

13.

*M*addalena wore her rebellion under a cloak of obedience, and she was proud of it. I was afraid to talk back to the teachers or even look the grown-ups in the eye when they talked to me, submitting to their reprimands without so much as an "I didn't do it on purpose."

She, however, remained defiant even in situations where she was made to apologize or say "Please." Humble and irreproachable on the outside, her rebellious instincts simmered just below the surface. When the teacher had to step out, the class leader—tasked with writing the names of those who'd misbehaved on the blackboard—would put Maddalena on top of the naughty list simply because she was the Cursed One, and "if she hasn't done anything wicked yet, she will soon enough." And still she refused to protest.

I wanted to stand up and say that it wasn't fair, but she'd shake her head—it would only make things worse. She knew the meanness of schoolgirls, whispered and devious, made of lies and rumors circulated behind your back, a meanness that would, however, sooner or later extinguish itself, like fire on dry grass.

And so Maddalena bore it all. The crumpled paper balls that hit her when they mocked her halting Latin, the stones they'd pelt her with in the yard as she shielded herself with her leather schoolbag. The worst were these five girls in the year above us, who had been in her class the previous year. Giulia Brambilla was the leader of the pack, the pharmacist's daughter Maddalena had punched, costing her a tooth. In the morning, Giulia was driven to school by her chauffeur in a black car, accompanied by her governess. She had fair, bouncy curls like the ones you'd see in fashion magazines, her obedient schoolgirl smile marred by the gap where her front tooth had been knocked out. She got good grades and was always polite and accommodating with the teachers. With Maddalena, however, she was shamelessly vicious: she'd throw handfuls of dirt at her, stuff half-chewed morsels of sandwiches into her pockets, yank her hair off her scalp, and call her "evil witch."

Maddalena never reacted, which made me angry. We should tell the teachers, I insisted, return the insults, make them pay. She was the one who'd given me a taste for rebellion, and I didn't understand why, now, she would put up with all that. "I promised," she'd say.

Giulia and her cronies were kind to me: they'd compliment my hair and ask if any of the boys were after me. That was the thing I hated most.

One day, as we were running around in the yard, Giulia tripped her and Maddalena fell. She hadn't even had a chance to put her hands forward to soften the fall, and ended up grazing her knees and chin.

"Does it hurt?" I asked as she wiped dust and gravel off her uniform.

Maddalena laughed, a laugh that grated like shoes on pebbles. "Not even a little bit." She didn't say a word to Giulia Brambilla, completely ignored her, as if she'd tripped and got hurt by herself. She still had to go see the nurse, however, because the blood wouldn't stop gushing out of her chin. It flowed through the fingers she pressed against the wound, staining her uniform.

As soon as she disappeared at the opposite end of the yard, I turned to face Giulia and her friends, who were still laughing:

"Why do you hate her so?" I asked, trying to imitate Maddalena's fierce tone.

"Who, her?" probed Giulia. "We don't hate her, you know."

"So why do you trip her, why do you throw stones at her, why are you so mean?"

"We're defending ourselves."

"Defending yourselves?"

"We're attacking her before she attacks us."

"Maddalena doesn't want anything from you!"

"Don't you know you mustn't speak her name? It's bad luck."

I swallowed. "Maddalena is my friend."

"The Cursed One doesn't have any friends. She simply can't."

The palms of my hands were sweaty, heart beating furiously in my ears.

"And do you know why?" insisted Giulia, blond curls lapping at her cheeks.

"Wh-why?" I realized I was stammering.

"Because anyone who gets close to her ends up getting hurt."

Behind her, her friends giggled, except for one, who sat quietly in a corner.

"That's not true," I bit back.

"Did she tell you about her brother?"

"Of course she did. He fell."

"Are you sure?"

"Of course!"

"And what about her father, did she tell you about him? And about Anna Tagliaferri?"

She must have noticed my confused expression. "Her father's leg got stuck in a press," she explained.

"I knew that," I said, willing my neck, shoulders, and legs to remember the defiant stance I'd adopt when we fought by the river with the Cursed Ones.

"And did you know that, that very morning, they'd had an argument and the Cursed One told him he might as well not come back?"

My throat went dry.

"And did you hear about Anna Tagliaferri?"

"No," I confessed.

"Didn't she tell you she made her bang her head on her desk until blood spurted out?"

"It was an accident."

"Ten times she banged her head. She wouldn't stop, like a hammer on a nail. Itala saw everything, they were in the same class in primary. Tell her, Itala."

The girl who kept to herself came forward. Crooked teeth, braids. She gave a small nod, shaking. Giulia crossed her arms over her chest and stared at me for a long moment. "Do you really want to fall out of a window or lose a leg?"

"No, I don't," I blurted out.

"Then you'd better stay away from her. The Cursed One's got the devil in her. And if the devil kisses you too, you'll have nowhere to run. Not even when you die, because you'll go to hell."

I was speechless, choking in anguish and guilt, my lips unable to shape a rebuttal. "You're vile," I wanted to say. "None of that is true, you lie!" Not a single word left my mouth. Why? Why couldn't I say what I thought, why did I keep swallowing it down until it lodged into my stomach and burned a hole in there?

"I bet her older brother's done for too. He's never coming back from the war. Going to be swallowed by the sands of Africa, I'm telling you!" She laughed, and her friends did too. All except for Itala, who was hiding again, behind Giulia, until one of the girls poked an elbow into her ribs and she let out a forced, choked burst of laughter. That's when I noticed Giulia hadn't been looking at me for a while, staring at a spot behind my back instead. I turned and saw Maddalena, a Band-Aid on her chin. The way she was looking at us frightened me.

Two days after that episode, Giulia Brambilla was found at the bottom of the stairs.

She'd fallen and split her forehead. She came round only after the doctors arrived and took her away, shrieking, face covered in blood, curls caked to her head. One of her shoes had slipped off her foot and was now precariously balanced on a step, forgotten. We were leaning over the second-floor banister, someone pointing at the dark stain on the marble steps, marred by the rescuers' footprints. From her portrait, Rosa Maltoni kept staring at the spot where Giulia had fallen. The flowers had wilted and gave off a nasty, rotten smell.

Our Italian teacher ordered us back into the classroom, but nobody listened. We were all gathered in the hallway, year-one girls in braids and final-year girls in fashionable hairdos, two groups that wouldn't normally mix.

"She was pushed," said a year-two girl with ribbons in her hair.

"She was definitely pushed," said our class leader.

"Who was it?"

"The Cursed One."

"Did anybody see anything?" asked a year-three girl.

"She couldn't have fallen by herself."

"It was the Cursed One, for sure."

"She's evil."

"She pushed her."

Voices piled up on top of each other, louder and louder, fighting to be heard over the bell the janitor kept ringing in the hope of restoring some order. I looked for Maddalena in the crowd, but I couldn't see her.

"Get back inside! Get back inside!" shouted the teacher as the girls pushed toward the stairwell, jostling to get to the front. Then, all of a sudden, silence.

Maddalena stepped forward like Jesus risen from the dead, and the crowd parted around her, instantly speechless. When she made it to the railing and looked down without saying a word, an unknown voice rose from the group:

"There she is. It was her. It was her!"

"Watch out or she'll push you down too!" warned another.

And another: "We must tell the teachers."

"Stay away from her! She'll curse you!"

"Why isn't she saying anything?"

"Don't let her touch you."

"She's sad because she wanted her dead. But she didn't manage to kill her."

"Now she'll have to find someone else to offer to the devil."

Maddalena turned. "It's not true!" She glared at the girls, one by one, ready to do battle.

The void around her grew wider, a few of the girls now peeling off from the group and walking toward the opposite end of the hallway, where the math and Latin teachers were finally succeeding in shepherding some of the year-one pupils into a classroom, aided by the janitor.

Maddalena seemed suddenly fragile, but fierceness still shone bright in her eyes. I wanted to reach out to her, walk to her, fill the empty space between us, say "I don't believe them," but I couldn't. It was as though I wasn't inside my body at all, but sitting a few steps back, watching myself watch her. Her eyes brought me back, and I could feel the floor under my feet again. She was looking for me. Around me, the girls' voices kept rising in a frenzied refrain: "She pushed her like she did with her brother. She's the one making these things happen!"

"Did you push her?" I blurted out. That question had shot up my throat in a quivering whisper that didn't belong to me, as if I was a puppet being maneuvered by someone else—someone scared and cowardly and mean, someone I never wanted to be.

Maddalena's face fell all of a sudden, her confidence gone. "Are you really asking me that?"

"You promised," I said, a slight tremor in my limbs.

The Cursed One's face crumpled as if she'd sucked on a lemon. "In the end you're just like all the rest." And she darted away, slashing a gap through the girls who jumped back, screaming.

I stood there, watching her, feeling weak, guilt fisting inside my stomach. "Maddalena!" I shouted. But she'd disappeared already.

I went looking for her while the others made their way back to the classrooms in neat two-by-two lines. The disappointment I'd read in her eyes burned inside of me as I rushed into the large, dingy room we used for recess when it was too cold to go outside. A fetid smell emanated from the toilet cubicles on either side, muffled sobs coming from my right.

"Maddalena?" I whispered, tentatively.

I followed that faint sound to the cubicle at the very end of the row.

"Maddalena, I'm sorry," I said, pushing the door open.

A huddled figure jolted in the dark, a thick shaft of light hitting her face. "Go away!"

I recognized the crooked teeth and mousy brown braids. "Itala? What are you doing in here?"

"I only wanted to scare her," she sobbed, the back of her head resting on the wall tiles. Her face was red from crying, nose running. Words came out in startled chunks. "I didn't do it on purpose, I swear!" She was wailing like a baby. "I couldn't take it anymore. Giulia is mean. But I didn't want her to die. I promise. I didn't!" She looked at me, eyes glinting with tears. "Don't tell anyone!" she begged. "Please, please don't tell anyone!"

"Stop crying. Crying is for idiots," I said before I shut the door.

I found Maddalena buried in the armchair outside the headmaster's office under the large portrait of the royal family, calm and collected, knees in a straight line. She saw me and immediately looked the other way.

"I know who did it."

"Why aren't you with the rest of the class?"

"It was Itala. She told me."

The Cursed One kept her eyes trained on a dusty print of ancient Roman ruins.

"Maddalena, come on!" I urged.

"So what?"

"We can tell the headmaster now, can't we?"

She laughed, a tense, wretched laugh: "They'll never believe *me*."

"What if I come with you?"

"You didn't believe me either."

"Merlini!" thundered a voice from inside the headmaster's office.

She stood, the soles of her shoes clacking on the floor, and turned her back to me.

"We're going in together," I insisted.

"You know nothing," she said, shaking, "They said it was me and that's how it's going to be."

"But it's not true!"

"They'll believe the truth they want to believe. The decision's been made, can't you see?"

I held my hand out, seeking hers. "I'm coming too. They'll believe me. They must."

She pulled back, flinching. "And who are *you*?" she said, a mean look flashing across her eyes. "I don't know you."

14.

*T*hat night, rain fell angry and gray, so thick you couldn't see past the sidewalk, and it didn't let up for days. The Lambro churned, bursting its banks. The water carried away the trees along the riverside, flooded basements, cracked cases of wine and old furniture, snaked under the bridges swelling with dark, silty sludge that left brownish marks on the stone pillars.

And all I could think was: *This is how it feels inside of me.*

Without Maddalena, my days dragged on squalid and meaningless, empty hours melting into each other. I hadn't kept my promise to Ernesto. I hadn't been there for her. Now, without her, I didn't feel whole anymore. I was naked, defenseless. Without her, the world around me withered.

We still sat together at school, but she wouldn't look at me. Her indifference was an icy grip that choked the air out of my lungs. If I offered to help her conjugate the Latin verbs the teacher had assigned to us, she'd shield her notebook with her arm without saying a word. The sandwich I gifted her every day (because she only ever had a slice of black bread) was still on my desk at the end of recess, untouched.

"I'm sorry, I'm sorry, I'm sorry"—I apologized a thousand ways. Nothing helped. So I'd hold my hand open, palm facing upward, and push the metal nib of my pen hard into the soft flesh until I drew blood. I'd show it to her, but she'd turn the other way. She'd always refused to play pretend, and now she pretended I didn't exist.

She didn't need me. She listened to our lessons, obsessively noted everything down, and remained at her desk reviewing her notes during recess. The teachers mostly ignored her because of what had happened with Giulia Brambilla, who in the meanwhile had come back to school sporting a bandaged head and crutches, although she refused to talk about the accident.

I'd taken to spying on the Cursed Ones in the afternoon, after school. I'd go to Leoni bridge and watch them from above, like I used to do not that many months before, in what felt like someone else's life now. I hoped they'd feel my gaze raking over them, but I was a ghost from the past, a forgotten shadow. Then I'd go home, my soul dragging at my heels, and lock myself up in my room, ignoring Carla's attempts to break through the walls I'd built around me. My mother was out almost every afternoon, and when she returned, the first thing she'd do was smile in the mirror and smooth her hair with her fingers. She never took any interest in me—mostly drifted around the house singing opera arias or compared her face to famous actresses in the magazines. If Carla asked for money for meat or milk, she'd leave it on the kitchen table the following morning without saying a word. I had the impression she was pretending to live alone. My father was worried about a delayed shipment of rabbit felt from Forlì.

Sometimes I'd sink my nails into my arms and scratch hard, trying to re-create the wounds inflicted by the cats over the summer. That pain obliterated the other pain, if only for a short time. And although nobody pointed at me on the street or called me "witch," I knew I was the one who deserved to be gnawed by the devil for all eternity. I felt the weight of the unspeakable sin I was hiding, same as when my brother had died. Maddalena trusted me and I'd betrayed her. I'd fancied myself brave, a hero from Greek mythology who could save her from anything, from fire, from the terrifying sea snake Hydra sprouting two new heads for each severed one. But I was guilty beyond redemption, and for a few horrible days, I wished I was dead.

15.

*T*oward the end of November, something happened that I'll never forget. When the time came for the morning salute, Maddalena remained seated, ignoring the teacher's reprimand, and declared, "I'm not getting up for that guy. Over my dead body."

Silence fell over the classroom, hot and sticky on the skin like sweat on a summer afternoon, when there's not a breath of wind and you melt even in the shade.

The duce. We'd been taught to love him since our first year of primary school, singing nursery rhymes that compared his birth to that of the baby Jesus and told the story of his life as though he was a saint. None of us had ever dreamed of questioning his existence or the sacred aura that surrounded him, and there was no reason to doubt the future would be any different from the present: the duce was immortal, he was always going to be there. The thought that he might not be was too scary to entertain. I didn't like the portraits that hung everywhere—his face had always reminded me of a big thumb. The other girls, however, said that he was handsome, that they wanted to marry him, and secretly kissed pictures of him they kept in their notebooks.

That said, I would never refuse to do the Fascist salute. It wasn't a matter of faith, respect, or admiration—it was simply habit, a social convention, same as saying "Good morning" and "Good evening." It was what was done, and there was nothing to be done about it. Maddalena, however, remained seated, her back stiff, and looked the teacher dead in the eye.

From my mother—who'd spoken to the modiste Luigia worked for—I'd heard that Ernesto's letters from the front were being heavily redacted. In some of them, all they could read was "I love you. Keep the faith." I'd also learned that a few days before, five carabinieri had turned up at Matteo Fossati's house. Oblivious to the tears and cries of his mother and sister, they'd taken away his father, who was to be sent into exile. It transpired that the previous night, full to the brim of cheap wine in a tavern, he'd blasphemed, which is to say, he'd been heard saying that Great Britain was right to punish Italy.

"Economic siege" we were supposed to call it. A few weeks prior to the incident, on November 18, the League of Nations had imposed economic sanctions on Italy following the start of the war in Ethiopia. And so it was that, while people sang *"Faccetta Nera"* and *"Ti saluto (vado in Abissinia),"* raving about the prosperity that the conquest of Ethiopia would bring to our country, the ban on exporting Italian products and importing war material had de facto crippled our entire economy. Posters on every street urged to "buy Italian," and walls were daubed with graffiti condemning the sanctions: "France and Great Britain have their empires, why can't Italy?" and "Long live Mussolini!" Carla would come back from the market with postcards stuffed in her shopping tote that read "I swear on my dignity as a Fascist and an Italian woman, not to buy foreign products, for me or for my family, ever again."

Matteo's father, however, kept saying, "All this war's good for is sending poor, honest boys to their death, and for what? A fistful of sand? The Abyssinians are right, I'm telling you. We're the ones who went looking for trouble in their homes! Because that's what these Fascists do. They take other people's stuff and pocket it, them and their cronies. They did it with my butcher shop and they'll do it to you too, you'll see. And us poor sods will be left with nothing, just some blasted sand from Ethiopia!" Someone at the tavern must have reported him, because not an hour after he'd gone home, the carabinieri tore him from his bed and dragged him away in his nightclothes.

Maddalena remained seated, fierce. In that posture, I saw the rebellious instincts that had never truly gone away finally burn to the surface, tired of hiding. Disappointment flashed across her face when the teacher simply replied, "As you prefer. We'll see what Mr. Ferrari has to say about your insubordination." As if the Cursed One was afraid of the headmaster.

After the salute, we sat and the lesson began. I had to close my eyes and take a deep breath before I could muster the courage to lean my head toward hers and whisper, "How are you?"

Maddalena jolted. "I'm fine.," she bit back.

Then I saw the look in her eyes. I'd seen it before: when we climbed the oak tree at the park not that long ago and she stared at the branches, determined to reach the top; when she shouted "Faster!" as we ran down a slope.

"Open your Italian grammar textbook to page forty-two." We were going to revisit the different types of verb phrases in a clause and then tackle the same concept in Latin grammar.

"Strada," the teacher called. "Stand up and read out the examples to the class, please."

"The duce is tireless," I recited in a firm, clear voice. "Tireless: adjective."

"The duce leads Italy," I continued. "Italy: noun."

"Excellent," said the teacher, tapping a ruler on the edge of her desk. "Now, would anyone like to translate into Latin?" she teased, knowing we still couldn't translate into Latin without a dictionary.

An unpleasant screech filled the room as Maddalena's desk scraped the floor. She stood at attention, cleared her throat, then began: *"Dux ducit Italiam in Erebo."* Then: *"Dux est scortum."*

The teacher blanched. All the blood seemed to have drained from her body into her toes.

"O-out!" she stuttered.

Maddalena stood still and didn't say a word. The rest of us were frozen, speechless.

"Out!" shouted the teacher. "Get out of here and don't come back!"

Maddalena bobbed a quick curtsy. "Yes, ma'am," she replied.

The other girls began whispering as she slowly made her way to the door like a queen to her coronation.

I stood too, so abruptly that my bag fell to the floor with a muffled thud. They all turned toward me—the girls, the teacher, even Maddalena, her hand already on the doorknob. She looked at me. It had been such a long time since I'd felt her eyes on me that my face burned as if I'd been standing by a fire.

Silence so thick you could touch it.

Breathing was suddenly hard. "We entrust the duce, the royal family, and the motherland to our Lord's care." I recited from the morning salute. Then I added: "I hope he sends them straight to hell."

The Cursed One waited for me and we left the room together, the teacher screaming herself hoarse, yelling that we deserved a good beating, that in the good old days it'd have been castor oil down our throats and someone coming to our house in the dead of night to knock our teeth out—and who'd get the last laugh then?

Maddalena shut the door, cutting out the screams. She walked to the window overlooking the yard, sat on the windowsill, and smiled at me. Wave after wave of heat washed over the void that had taken residence inside me, and I felt like crying.

God, how I'd missed her.

"You shouldn't have done that," she said. "Do you know what's going to happen now?"

"No. And I don't care."

"You don't care?"

"No."

"I couldn't take it anymore," she blurted. "I couldn't pretend anymore. It's all so wrong. Don't you see?"

"See what?"

"The war and the salute and saying what they want us to say and thinking what they want us to think. Following the rules, being good girls . . ." she caught her breath. "I'm tired of repeating their words. Ernesto always said, 'Words matter, Maddalena. You can't say them without thinking, otherwise they become dangerous.' And he's right. But words can also be powerful, don't you think?"

I swallowed my fear and asked, "What did you say earlier in class? It was Latin and I'm not sure I understood."

She threw her head back and laughed. "I said the duce is a whore."

Part III

The

TEST

of

TRUE

COURAGE

16.

"Nobody can know about this."

That was the first thing Mom said after leaving the headmaster's office. She wore heavy makeup, a turquoise hat with a birdcage veil, and an evening gown—completely inappropriate for the occasion—which she kept smoothing as she nodded like an obedient schoolgirl (since I'd been anything but). The headmaster droned on about my "rash display of anti-Italian sentiment," and I stood with my back against the wall, fingers interlaced. I wasn't to make a sound: my mother would speak for me. "Ours is a respectable family, we want nothing to do with this whole story."

Finally the headmaster's office door closed behind us, and we were alone. Mom dragged me to the portrait of the royal family and stopped, looking at me as if she wanted to crush me under her heel, stressing again that I wasn't to breathe a word about this to anyone.

"Let me explain . . ."

"Shut up!" she shouted. "Just shut up! Do you seriously not understand?" She shook her head, gold earrings knocking against her cheeks. "Do you know what happens to a girl when her reputation is ruined? She might as well drown herself in the river!"

"I only wanted to . . ."

"What? What did you want?"

"To be heard."

"Wretched girl!" Her hand started toward me and I flinched, expecting a slap. Instead, she grabbed my chin. "Your job is to keep quiet. And wait. That's what a good girl is supposed to do."

"Wait for what?"

She shrugged, a cruel smirk I couldn't explain twisting her lips. "You'll understand when you grow up." Her hand lingered on my face, as if she wanted to caress me but had forgotten how. "And if your father *still* wants to pretend nothing's happened, this time I'll take matters into my own hands and bury this story for good. For all of us."

Once home, Dad didn't say a word. His hard stare landed on me, then he looked away. At dinner he was curt and testy, leaving the table without finishing his soup. The following morning, as he was about to leave the house, my mother blocked the door, arms folded across her chest. "Enough. You must say something to *your daughter!*" His gaze lingered on me for a long time, the same hard stare as the previous evening. They weren't his eyes, that wasn't my father.

"Well?" my mother insisted.

"Your mother wants me to scold you," he began, "but I can't be bothered."

Mom doubled over, screaming for Carla to fix her a tonic because her head was killing her. She ran into the kitchen, still yelling. "I just can't with this madhouse!"

"I'll say this, however," my father continued. "As you grow up, you'll learn that often, it pays not to say what you really think."

"And how do you do that?"

"You keep your thoughts inside. Guard them. Polish them. In there, they're safe."

"And will it stop hurting so much?"

He smiled a tired smile. "No. That it never does."

Eventually I was readmitted to school. My mother paraded around the house saying, "You'll do well to remember that your father cares nothing for *his daughter's* reputation." It was thanks to her that I'd been allowed back. She only said she'd asked for a favor from a friend of Dad's, someone important, and that it was all sorted. None of the teachers mentioned that episode again, as if it had never happened. The other girls shunned me. They threw stones at me in the yard and called me "the radical."

Maddalena, on the other hand, had been expelled without much fanfare. The kind of disobedience she had displayed didn't even bear discussing. I should have been grateful to my mother, seeing as it was only thanks to her intervention that I wouldn't have to repeat the year. And yet the only place I really wanted to go back to was the Cursed One's gang. I'd mentioned it to Maddalena. "Are you sure you're brave enough?" she'd asked me.

She wanted to see if I was still worthy of them.

Matteo and Filippo told her to get rid of me, that I was poison. "Fool me once . . ." repeated Matteo, who had adopted more and more of his father's sayings since he'd been taken away. Maddalena answered that she could watch out for herself, and she wasn't one to be fooled. The best way to ensure forgiveness was to put me to the test.

It was cold on the evening of the test of true courage—the cold that slashes your cheeks and thickens your breath into fog. The streetlamps flickered on as ladies wrapped in fox fur stoles hurried home after the latest round of shopping.

"Keep your head down," the Cursed One whispered to me. We were crawling on the greengrocer's marble floor, just after closing time. Yellow light from the streetlamps poured in from the shop windows. The glass panes were rimmed in frost, ice crystals creeping inward from the scuffed wood at the corners. Hazy marks stood out where children had pressed their noses against the windows to peek at the trays of dates and candied ginger. The mushy scent of beans hit my nostrils, followed by spikes of zingy citrus. Tresoldi sang *"Parlami d'amore Mariù"* at the back of the shop as he went over the books, his voice muffled by the frosted glass on the closed door. From the backyard came the frantic barking of the chained dog.

The Cursed One crawled in front of me. I could see her ragged skirt, the frayed hem of her old coat, the worn soles of her shoes. A bitter chill from the marble floor seeped through the sleeves of my sweater as the acrid taste of fear invaded my mouth. I took a deep breath, Maddalena's words resonating in my mind: "Me? I'm not afraid of anything."

We had snuck in just as Maria, the Colombos' maid, had triggered the bell over the door on her way out, her sturdy farmer's arms laden with shopping bags. We'd hidden behind the empty wooden crates piled up in a corner, where we could see without being seen. Tresoldi had retired to the back of the shop to tally the day's takings and the room had gone quiet as a hollow tree, the sign on the door announcing, "We're closed."

Maddalena had looked at me then, her eyes calm and confident: "Are you ready?"

We'd left our hiding place and begun crawling across the icy floor. I thought of Tresoldi's face, of his large hands scarred by artichoke thorns, of the dirt under his fingernails, and fear gripped my throat again.

He was kind when I visited the shop with my mother and she ordered fuzzy peaches and potatoes, cauliflower and walnuts, even strawberries in the summer. He'd feign interest in whatever she was saying, even though it was the same conversation every week. Then he'd laugh and ask me if I was enjoying school or if I fancied a peppermint, disappearing into the back to fetch one without waiting for an answer. I always thanked him so he wouldn't get offended like Mom had taught me, then popped the mint into my mouth, saying, "Very nice." I'd spit it out as soon as we left. Every time Mom opened her purse to settle half the bill in advance, Tresoldi would nod politely, looking pleased. When he was angry, however— especially with his son, Noè, if he'd happened to trip on a crate of tomatoes or get the change wrong—I could hear him from the other side of the street: cursing, the sound of things being smashed, faces being slapped. It frightened me.

The greengrocer sang in the back room now, right behind the locked door, lamplight filtering through the frosted-glass pane. Maddalena jerked her chin. The clementines crate was at the back of the shop, near the cash register. Clementines were a precious, coveted fruit that Maddalena and the Cursed Ones would only come by on Christmas Day, as a present, and never more than one each— some because they really couldn't afford them, others as a lesson in discipline and sacrifice. They weren't that rare in my house, truth be told. Mom would buy a bag as soon as the temperatures dipped, even though they were expensive, and Dad said she was spoiling me, and spoilt children made for weak adults. I'd never tell the Cursed Ones, however, because they'd call me a "blister," a pain in the neck, bothersome as a fly.

We crawled to the crate we had our eyes on, Maddalena first, me right behind. She slowly rose to her feet, cautious as a snail pricking up its antennae and slithering out of its shell as the first raindrops hit the ground.

"That's it," she said, holding up the hem of her skirt with one hand while the other grabbed the clementines and dropped them in the hollow she'd created. As the fruits piled in, she held the skirt tighter and tighter against her chest so they wouldn't spill out, exposing strong, pale thighs.

The greengrocer was still singing. I shot up and started filling my pockets too, then stuffed two clementines in my panties. Laughter bubbled on the Cursed One's lips, but she held it back, a stifled rasp dying in her throat.

That's when we heard the bell, signaling the door had been opened behind us. I went stiff all over as Noè's silhouette sliced through the yellow light from the streetlamp across the street. He was just back from his deliveries, carrying three empty crates. I let out a cry. Maddalena clamped a hand over my mouth, releasing her skirt and dropping the clementines, which went rolling all over the floor. They sounded like the stones we'd send tumbling into the river when we chased each other on the banks of the Lambro.

"Who's there?" Tresoldi called out.

Maddalena yanked my arm. I could not move. Noè bent over to pick up a clementine that had ended up next to his shoe, and Maddalena pressed a finger to her lips: "Shush!" Then she pushed me behind the crates of fruit near the entrance, wedged against the zucchini display case by the window.

"What's all this racket then?" the greengrocer kept shouting as he emerged from the room at the back. Maddalena pressed her face to the slits in the crates. I could feel my pulse hammering at my temples.

"What have you done?" yelled Tresoldi. "You damn fool!!"

I peeked through the slits too.

Tresoldi's apron, covered in dirt and streaks of dark juice, had been tossed to the floor. He bent over and picked up a clementine. No longer a shiny, flawless sphere, the bruised fruit gave in like dough when you press a thumb into it.

"You lout!" he yelled, lobbing it at Noè.

Then he started forward, his bad foot trailing behind while the other stomped furiously, so hard the floor shook. Tresoldi grabbed his son's arm and smacked his face, his hand landing with a wet whack like a mallet pounding a slab of raw meat. Noè fell, elbows and chin hitting the marble floor hard, clementines squashed under his belly. Tresoldi kept calling him an idiot and kicking his side, holding on to the wall to steady his bad leg.

Noè tried to peel himself off the floor, blood streaming from his nose, and his eyes found ours through the slits of the empty crates. I squeezed Maddalena's hand. Soon it would be our turn. Any minute now Noè would tell on us, and his father would smack us raw and kick us until our ribs broke.

But nothing happened. Noè pressed his forehead to the floor.

"Now clean up this mess!" ordered Tresoldi, then he disappeared behind the frosted-glass door, kicking clementines as he went, as though all his rage had gathered into his shoes, into his toeless foot.

Noè swiped a finger under his nose, painting a red streak over his knuckles. Maddalena's hand felt cold and dry in mine. Suddenly she sprang forward, dragging me out of our hiding place. Noè looked at us.

"Wait!" I whispered, but she picked up a clementine and pushed me through the door. Outside, I could almost taste snow in the cold air.

17.

*T*he following day, Maddalena made two important deci-
sions.

The first: I had passed the test, and we could be friends
again. The second: she had a debt to pay, and she would repay it at all
costs. That afternoon she came to collect me at home and confessed
she'd stolen the money her mother had been stashing in her "secret
place," that is, her father's old lunch box. She showed me a crumpled
fifty lira note.

"And what do you plan to do with that?"

"I want to give it to Noè."

"What if your mother finds out?"

"I don't care."

"You don't care if she finds out you've stolen from her secret
place?"

"I said I don't."

We stood waiting for him on the pavement opposite his shop,
next to the tobacconist's. "Long live the duce!" "For Italy!" "No
sanctions!" shouted the graffiti on the shutter behind us. I blew on
my hands to stave off the cold: "How much longer do we have to
wait?"

"As long as it takes."

As soon as Noè stepped out and began tying the crates to the rack on his bike, Maddalena said, "Come on," and rushed across the street, stopping in front of him. I joined her, panting, my mouth dry. He shot us a look, then resumed his task. His hands were big, a grown man's hands, with calloused fingers and beautiful, round nails.

"This is for you," Maddalena said, holding out the note to him.

"What's that?"

"Money. For the clementines," she answered. "And for your nose and your face too."

"Where did you get it?"

"That's none of your business."

He looped the strap around the crates and hooked it to the rack. One of his cheeks was swollen, a bruise the color of ripe plums blossoming under his right eye.

Maddalena's arm was still stretched toward him.

"I don't want it."

"Don't you know who I am? Don't you know what I'll do to you? Take it, I said!"

"You're Mrs. Merlini's daughter," Noè answered.

She gave a little nod.

"Put it away."

"Why don't you want the money?"

"Put it back, Maddalena," he insisted, tugging at the crate to check it was secured properly. "Before your mother finds out and before my father comes back. He still remembers you from the time you stole the cherries."

"You think I'm afraid of your father? I'm not afraid of anything."

Noè gripped the handlebars, pushing the pedal down. He looked at me and I fought the impulse to lower my gaze. "You could give me an IOU, if you want."

"What's that?"

"Something grown-ups use when they need to pay for something, but they don't have the money. So they write 'I owe you' on a piece of paper."

"But I do have the money."

"And I don't want it."

"What do you want then, if not money?"

"I don't know," he said. "I haven't decided yet." He hopped on the saddle and started pedaling, disappearing into Via Vittorio Emanuele and then across Leoni bridge, the crates teetering behind him.

Only after Noè had dropped out of sight, swallowed by the crowd in Piazza Duomo, Maddalena stashed the fifty lira note back into her pocket. "Did you hear what he said?"

"That he doesn't want the money."

"Not that. The other thing."

"And what did he say?"

"He said my name."

18.

Pressed against the parapet on Leoni bridge, we watched the swollen river surge past the highest notch on the pillars. "I can really make bad things happen to people, you know." Maddalena said.

"Stop testing me!" I blurted out.

"No," she cut me off. "I mean it. The things Giulia Brambilla told you that day, about my brother and my father and even Anna Tagliaferri—it's all true."

She told me about the first time she realized she had what she called "the voice." She was seven, playing with Dario in their kitchen. Her brother was only four and she was like a queen to him. Anything she did, he wanted to do too. That day they were playing at being swallows: they'd stand on a chair and jump down, pretending to be fledglings who were learning to fly. Then Maddalena had told Dario, "You've got this now! You can even fly up in the sky if you want to."

And he'd climbed on the table, leaning out of the window, and jumped. He hadn't fallen. He'd spread his arms wide, turned to her, and said, "Watch me!"

The Cursed One was quiet now, looking at her feet. I pictured her smaller, so small I could cradle her in my hand, alone in a silent kitchen, holding her breath, bracing for the impact.

"Is that why you're afraid?"

"I'm not afraid."

"You're afraid to play pretend, I mean. To tell stories."

"When I tell stories, sometimes the stories come true." She hesitated. "Or maybe it's people who feel those stories all over them and do bad things. Like Dario, who jumped out of a window because he believed he could fly. He believed it because I told him."

"It wasn't your fault."

"And whose fault was it then?"

"I don't know." I shrugged. "Maybe it just happened. Bad things happen and that's that."

I thought of my brother who had died when he was tiny and soft, of my mother who'd spent the night praying to the Lord not to take him, and said: "People die every day for no reason, even if you pray for them not to die. And it's nobody's fault."

"That doesn't work for me," she snapped. Then she told me of the time when she was ten and she'd argued with her father over something silly: a shoelace she'd used to play with her spinning top and ended up tearing. Her father was angry because he'd have to go to work with a loose shoe, and he'd punished her. She told me how that night, before he'd sent her to bed without her dinner, she'd said to him: "You'd better not come back tomorrow."

She told me about Anna Tagliaferri, who sat next to her in her final year of primary school. Of how she'd banged her head on the desk until blood gushed out, mixing with the spilled ink, and froth gathered at her mouth. All because they'd argued, and she'd told Anna she "didn't want to see her anymore."

It was as if, in the midst of all these tragedies and deaths, she'd somehow found solace in the absurd belief that she was the one who'd brought them about.

"So, if you told me to jump into the river and drown right now, I'd do it?"

She buried her neck in her shoulders.

"Just like that?"

"Sometimes that's all it takes," she said. "Other times I have to explain it to you. Convince you it's real. As if it was you doing the thinking. Do you see?"

"Try."

"Try what?"

"Try it now. With me."

"No." She grimaced, eyes like a pinhead.

"I trust you," I pressed her. "Really. I just want to understand . . ."

"No!" she shouted. "I don't want to do that anymore. Especially not to you."

"You don't just make bad things happen," I countered.

She looked at me but didn't answer.

"The other day, at school," I continued, "it was only because of you that I stood up. And I enjoyed it. Even if I was scared. Scared to death. But it was beautiful. Afterward, I mean, once I was home. And I don't care what my mother thinks. I wouldn't have cared if they'd never let me go back to school."

"Don't say that."

"I felt good. Lighter. Like when you stay under water too long, holding your breath, and then you come up for air. Also, the first time I bled, you're the one who made the fear go away."

"That's different."

"I didn't think I could do that."

"Do what?"

"Rebel," I answered. "You taught me how."

She dangled her legs over the river again.

"Why aren't you afraid, huh?"

I hesitated. In the days Maddalena had disappeared from my life I had realized how strong our bond was. But I couldn't find the words to tell her. *Love* was a word grown-ups used indiscriminately, especially in school when they talked about Mussolini. They told us he "loved children" and asked if we loved him back. That's the term they'd use, *love.* And then there were others, like *burn, die, suffer.* Love was cinema actresses gripping curtains—something acted out, something fake.

So I said, "I care about you."

After a while, I realized Maddalena was crying.

19.

December had always been a month I'd eagerly awaited. From the moment Carla turned the page on the calendar hanging next to the ice box in the kitchen, I'd start counting down the days until Christmas. I'd mark an X with my crayons at the end of each day, willing away the hours that separated me from the honey roast with chestnuts, from the presents, from racing down the slopes at Villa Reale Park on our sleds.

That year I barely noticed. December came, and with it dirty snow shoveled carelessly from the roads, left to rot in the gutters. In the shops, the cheerful advertisements with children devouring large slices of Motta panettone were replaced by muted, austere propaganda posters with a single slogan: "A Motta Christmas is an Italian Christmas."

Outside the grocery shops and after the 11 a.m. service, old ladies muttered about the war that wouldn't end. The men stood to one side on their own—old men with crooked backs who spat chewing tobacco on the snow, railing against God and what they called "the great indignity." It was the United Kingdom's fault, and France's— hypocrites who flaunted their empires and colonized whichever African countries they pleased, while we couldn't even get real tea anymore and my mother had to stoop to hibiscus tea.

In school, our history teacher had hung a map of Ethiopia on the wall, where we were supposed to pin flags marking the territories we'd conquered. Our army marched forward and we had to say a Hail Mary and Our Father for our "brave soldiers." Maddalena's desk had remained empty. She said she didn't care, but I knew that in her letters to Ernesto she still wrote about lessons and tests, which she'd learn about from me. She'd made Donatella and Luigia promise not to say anything and they'd agreed, so he wouldn't have to worry about that too.

Maddalena said they'd devised a secret code with Ernesto: he'd mark the words he meant for her to read with an ink stain, so he could tell the truth without being censored: "*I don't want* to complain. I've learnt *to fight* and it's really not difficult *anymore*. I like *the food here*—what *is appalling* is the incompetence of *these people* on the other side. There *aren't* braver men than my comrades in arms, risking their lives every day to defeat *the enemy*." At the bottom, in his neat, almost childlike handwriting, the same recommendations each time: "Do try and behave yourself. Look after Donatella and Luigia. Keep the faith."

"Put on something nice. And wrap up warm, it's cold outside," ordered my mother on December 18.

"Do we have to go?"

"We must."

"But why?"

"Because it cannot be helped."

We left the house and headed for Piazza Trento, joining the crowds gathered under the war memorial. I was straining to find Maddalena, but my mother kept dragging me forward, gripping my wrist: "Keep moving!"

Then I froze, planting my heels firmly on the ground, and yanked my arm free: "Let go of me!"

She looked at me as people jostled us to move forward, and we stared at each other like strangers. She swiped two fingers under her nose, runny from the cold. "What did you say?" Her eyes flashed with a thousand warnings about my reputation and our good name: people would judge me, good girls never disobey their parents.

But I wasn't my father, and I couldn't keep it all in anymore. "Let go of me, please." I ran away and didn't look back.

When I finally reached Maddalena, she asked, "What's the matter with you?"

"I was afraid I wouldn't find you," I answered, panting. We watched as the old ladies struggled up the steps that led to a bronze statue of warriors locked in battle under the watchful eye of an archangel. They were going to donate their wedding bands for the glory of the motherland and our Lord.

Little mounds of gray snow littered the square. White flecks dappled the archangel's trumpet and the shields of the bronze warriors piled on top of each other. Representatives of the *Combattenti e Reduci* veterans' association held their banners high, while the traffic wardens carried the standard with the city's coat of arms, the iron crown. The authorities were all in attendance, well dressed and standing guard next to the upturned helmet where the women would deposit their wedding bands, inches from the names of those who had lost their lives in that war they called "great." Mom's brother had fought in it too.

I remembered the times my father had made me climb to the highest point on the monument—although you weren't supposed to—and read me the names of the dead soldiers. I pretended that they were friends of mine, that war was just a game. I imagined them rolling to the ground after being shot from the tip of a classmate's finger, then springing back to their feet and going home for their afternoon snack. It was odd to think that a person who'd had a name and a surname was now gone, nothing but fading letters in the rain.

Dad had explained that the base of the monument hid a secret chamber protected by a gate, and in it were two small bottles containing water and sand from the Piave River. A sacred river, he said. A song had been written about that river. Before we headed back, he would always stop by the entrance to the chapel and read the inscription out loud: "And here the mothers will come / and show their young the path you marked in blood." They were the words of a poet who loved our country, and he meant to say that those boys hadn't died in vain, because Italians would always remember them—although I wasn't so sure my father believed that.

I told Maddalena, who replied, "Nobody cares about those men giving their lives. Everyone's forgotten about the old war, or they only remember it when it pays to do so. All they talk about is the new war, can't you see?"

One by one, women in their Sunday best, hair tucked under a headscarf, climbed the steps and dropped their wedding bands into the helmet. In return, each was given an iron band engraved with "Gold to the Motherland" and a diploma emblazoned with a wheat sheaf. In the crowd, people raised their arms in the Fascist salute, perhaps as an excuse to move and keep the cold at bay.

Maddalena kept running her tongue on her cracked lips. "This is not what believing in God is about," she kept repeating.

My mother wore a hat with a golden ribbon and white gloves. I pointed her out to Maddalena in the crowd. "Look how she's preening." Back straight, wrapped in her fur-trimmed coat, she climbed the steps to the helmet. But I knew she'd be donating a fake ring, a gold-plated one she'd commissioned from Viganoni, the goldsmith.

Maddalena's mother's headscarf flapped in the wind. "They can't take this away too," she whined, stroking her scuffed wedding band. This time, however, she couldn't argue that Mussolini would set things right "if only he knew," because it was the duce himself who had asked Italian women to sacrifice their gold. "No respect," she repeated. "There's no respect left."

"She doesn't *have* to do it, you know?" Maddalena whispered in my ear. "No one's forcing her."

But I knew it wasn't that simple. My father had explained it to me that morning, while Mom rubbed the surface of the new, fake ring with a nail file to make it look worn. That day, people hadn't gathered in response to a direct order, one of those orders that would earn you a shot in the back if you disobeyed it, or have your name struck from the ranks of "the honorable." A "spontaneous gesture" they called it. If you refused, you might not get a bullet between your shoulder blades, but you'd still have to watch your back. Even the queen had donated her wedding band, as had Rachele Mussolini. The famous playwright Pirandello had donated his Nobel medal, the poet D'Annunzio a whole crate of gold. All good citizens would surely follow their example.

Maddalena rubbed her palms together, fingers numb from the cold. I took off my gloves and began massaging her hands with mine. "Put them in my pockets, that'll warm them up." She hugged me, and the cold seemed to melt away when I felt her breath on my neck.

Her mother slogged up the steps wrapped in a black dress and black shawl: a shivering swallow. She stood a few inches from the altar for a long moment, struggling to remove the ring. A boy bent down and wet his fingers in the snow, then took her hand and massaged her fingers until the band slid off. He didn't toss it in the helmet himself, however: he held it out to her and stepped back, tipping his hat and bowing as a show of respect. Baffled, Maddalena's mother stared at him, then kissed the ring and dropped it in the helmet with the rest.

At that moment, Donatella spotted us in the crowd and started off toward us, arm in arm with Tiziano. Her cheeks burned from the cold but she was perfectly coiffed. "I came to donate the gold chain from my confirmation."

"Ladies—good morning to you," said Tiziano with that smile that belonged on a Greek statue.

"What about you? Didn't you bring anything?" Donatella inquired, fussing with her hair. Then she turned to Maddalena. "You have that gold charm you got for your first communion. You should have thought about that."

Maddalena shrugged and I did the same.

"Ah, come now, they're only little girls," Tiziano cut in. "What difference would they make? Let's go," he concluded, hugging his girlfriend close.

As they walked away, I noticed his fingers slipping between the buttons of her coat.

"Stop! They'll see us." Donatella giggled.

Before the crowd swallowed them, I heard Tiziano say, "Didn't I promise I'd marry you?" and she let him kiss her hair, her cheeks, her neck.

20.

Only two days to go until Christmas and snow was coming down thick, seemingly determined to blanket and hide everything from view. We had the park near the tram stop to ourselves, and an odd silence enveloped us, magnifying all smells: woolen gloves soaked from our snowball fight, sweat seeping through our heavy coats, sticky pine sap. Dangling her legs from a swing, the Cursed One kicked at the mounds of snow in front of her while Filippo and Matteo, propped up against the wooden frame, talked about presents and the war.

"When I grow up, I want to go," said Filippo, "so I can learn to fire a rifle, and steal the enemy's women." That year, he was hoping his father would gift him a tin train and a real rifle, with real bullets—then, at the Saturday rallies, everyone would see he could shoot like a man. Matteo, for his part, simply hoped he could see his own father again, who hadn't written home from his exile because he'd never even learned to read. The two boys fought often since Matteo's father had been arrested, over the silliest of things—whose turn it was to push the Cursed One on the swings, for instance, or who'd get to eat the only intact biscuit in the bundle Filippo had smuggled out of his kitchen in a handkerchief embroidered with his initials. They'd shout and call each other mean names. Matteo said that when he grew up,

Filippo would be just like the carabinieri who'd taken his father: a traitor and a coward. Filippo said Matteo was an idiot and when he grew up he'd be a nobody like his father. Then they'd come to blows, rolling in the snow, kicking. Maddalena would separate them, shouting "Enough!" "You're just repeating what other people say," she'd continue, smacking them both around the head. Because it was her asking, they'd eventually, begrudgingly make peace. There was only one thing Matteo and Filippo never argued about: nothing but war could make a man out of you, because you hadn't really grown up until you'd seen blood being spilled.

Maddalena wore her old men's coat buttoned up to her chin. She drew a circle in the snow with the tip of her foot. "You don't need to go to war to be a man."

"What about honor?" asked Filippo.

"You can have honor without a war. And without the duce," she bit back.

Matteo buried his hands under his arms to warm them up and sniffled. "I don't give a toss about the duce. But if you want to call yourself a man, you have to be able to kill, war or not."

"These are man things," Filippo added. "What do you know about that, huh?"

Suddenly, silence fell. A heap of snow slid from a branch near the top of a tree and landed with a thud. Since the bleeding incident down at the Lambro, Matteo and Filippo had begun eyeing us suspiciously, always looking for things that would set them apart from us. And ever since Maddalena had brought me back despite their reservations, they'd taken to whispering to each other animatedly, then stopping as soon as we came near, claiming they were discussing "man things." They were convinced we were hiding something from them, and therefore, not to be outdone, they'd endeavored to come up with a secret of their own.

"Are you saying you two could kill someone?" Maddalena taunted them.

"You don't believe we could?" Matteo bit back.

"What does she know anyway?" A mean laughter burst out of Filippo's throat. "She's only saying that because she can't go to war, not even when she grows up, and she has to stay here and find a husband and give him sons who can become soldiers. My brother told me—the only thing females are good for is giving without asking for anything in return, like the duce's women. Because if you're a man, the things you want, why you just go and grab them. Like Dad always says."

All of a sudden Maddalena jumped down from the swing and started toward him. Filippo backed off so fast he tripped over the wooden pole and fell, his back sinking in the snow.

"You're afraid now, aren't you?" The Cursed One was calm.

Filippo panted, his arms spread wide, breath steaming out of his gaping mouth. "Hit me then. What are you waiting for?"

"No need," she replied "You already know I'd beat you."

"You've let that traitor change you!" he said as he rose to his feet, brushing snow off his coat. And for a moment there, looking in his blue eyes, I saw his father's—that way he had of looking at things like they belonged to him. "You're only girls. What do you know about killing?" he hissed.

It was the first time one of them had used that word for Maddalena: she had never been a *girl*. Not to them.

"You're the little girls. You know nothing!" Maddalena spat on the ground and grabbed my hand. "Let's go." We ran together toward the gate, snow crunching under our shoes.

"Feed a stray once and before you know it, he'll be stealing your dog's dinner!" Matteo shouted at our backs—one of his father's sayings again. As if the Cursed One belonged to them and I was an enemy come from God knows where to snatch her away and keep her all to myself.

Maddalena held my hand the whole time as we headed toward the bridge. Street vendors peddling roasted chestnuts and chestnut flatbreads huddled in street corners, thick smoke rising in the sky from their stoves. The shop windows were foggy with the breaths of women hurrying through their final purchases, and when the doors opened, war songs drifted out from the radios. The water in the fountains had frozen over, the Lambro was as gray as the sky.

When we got to Leoni bridge, Maddalena stopped. She was panting, her cheeks flaming from all the running. "We're going to eat panettone with custard after the Christmas mass," she said. "I told Donatella to save you a slice. If you want to join us, we'll be at the midnight service in San Gerardino."

The midnight service was a grown-up thing that had always been out of bounds for me. It was unseemly for a child to be awake at that hour, my mother argued, but the truth was that she wanted to parade around without having to worry about me. It was a way to flaunt what you had to the whole town, the Christmas mass. People went to see and be seen, and to bad-mouth those who weren't there. In the cathedral, the best seats were reserved: the regional party representative with his entire family, all in uniform, took up the front bench. Right behind them were the mayor, the city council members, and the carabinieri: on Christmas Eve, the first three rows were solid black.

That night, my mother walked into my room and found me already in bed, blankets pulled all the way to my chin, lights off. "Get up. You're a woman now. This year you'll be accompanying us to church. And mind you, don't fall asleep, that would be highly inappropriate."

"I-I have to get dressed," I managed to reply, shocked. I was, however, already dressed. I was lying in bed in my stockings, skirt, and blouse so I could sneak out and join Maddalena. Instead, I had to get up and leave with my parents.

Outside, the sky was black as ink, frost hung in the air, and a cold glow from the Christmas lights bathed the silent, icy streets. "Stand up straight!" my mother snapped when we arrived in Piazza Duomo. In the brief stretches of silence between the bell tolls, the ladies' heels clacked against the cobblestones while the gentlemen huddled outside the cathedral, smoking cigars and talking about money, women, and the war.

Inside, the smell of incense was so strong it made me nauseous, the dark notes of the organ swallowing the sharp words of those who saw a coveted seat snatched from under their noses. We sat on a bench in the fourth row, behind the Colombos, who were out in force: Mr. and Mrs. Colombo, Tiziano and Filippo. Tiziano spun toward us and smiled at me, then kept singing in Latin, facing the altar. He had a marvelous voice, and a thought crossed my mind: that's what the angels who sat beside the Lord in heaven must look like.

The priest in his golden vestments talked about God, the motherland, family. His words felt rehearsed, made up—a performance, a puppet show.

I remained standing after the Glory hymn. My father looked at me but said nothing. "Sit down," my mother hissed. "Sit down this instant!" I was the only person standing, everyone was silent. All you could hear were the priest's words and the final notes of the organ echoing faintly down the aisle. If I left, the whole town would see me.

"I'm sorry," I told my father. "I have to go." I squeezed out of the bench and broke into a run down the central aisle, not caring if I stepped on the black marble tiles that sent you straight to hell. I burst out, wind slashing the exposed skin on my face. The square was silent, and dark, and full of cold. Darting down Via Vittorio Emanuele, I crossed Leoni bridge and continued along the Lambro, stopping after San Gerardino bridge. The church cloister was dark, and you could barely make out the muffled voices joined in an a cappella hymn.

I pushed the door open. The church was small and dimly lit.

I spotted Maddalena in the second-to-last row, sitting with Donatella, Luigia, and Mrs. Merlini. "I thought you weren't coming," she said as she saw me.

I was warm and out of breath.

"Did you run all the way here?" Maddalena laughed. "Come and sit."

Donatella shuffled closer to her mother to make room for me.

"Merry Christmas," said Luigia.

Mass at the cathedral was a ceremony meant to impress. It was for those who cared nothing for God, and only worried about making a show of their faith for the benefit of the dignitaries in the front rows, singing better and louder than everyone else. Mass in San Gerardino was meant to be listened to, it was for those who really needed the comfort of religion.

Even Maddalena dropped to her knees for the Holy Communion prayer. She communicated with God in her own way, as if he was sitting right next to her rather than all the way up in heaven. She was determined to believe, and once she'd made a decision, there was no changing her mind. Perhaps talking to God made her feel closer to Ernesto—she knew that, somewhere, he was doing the same.

The marble under the benches was slick with the melted snow people had tracked in under their shoes. "This is a night of hope," the priest said, and I leaned ever so closer to Maddalena, then dropped to my knees and rested my chin on my interlaced fingers. I tried to pray. I prayed for Ernesto and for the war to end soon. For Dad's hat factory and even for my mother. I prayed for my brother, who was gone, and for what he could have become if he'd survived. And I prayed for Maddalena. When I was with her, I could believe the most outlandish of notions, such as the idea that the Lord loved me too, despite the sin I was hiding. It was her who made me believe I could be saved too. It was her who lit everything up.

It was past one o'clock by the time we reached the Merlinis' house. I'd never been up so late, and tiredness seemed to pulse at the back of my neck, dulling my thoughts and making me feel older. We sat at the bare kitchen table—there was no tablecloth. Luigia had started opening the blue box containing the panettone while Donatella fetched the glass bowl with the mascarpone custard. Her movements were slow, as if weighed down by an invisible load, and she spoke little, only to answer "yes" or "no" to her mother's questions.

It was odd being in a house with no men. It felt emptier, quieter. The smell of wet dirt still permeated the place since Luigia had taken to smoking rolled-up cigarettes with the cheap tobacco Ernesto was partial to. She took out the panettone and offered me a slice. *Pan del Toni*, she called it, Toni's bread. Legend had it that a baker called Toni who worked for the Sforzas, Milan's ancient ruling family, had created the sweet bread to cover up a mistake. "Let me know if you like it," she said, her voice brittle and sad as she spooned some custard onto my plate.

Luigia picked up the cardboard cylinder that had been wrapped around the panettone and placed it on Donatella's head like a crown. "Come on—it's meant to be good luck!"

A faint smile touched Donatella's lips. "Thank you," she said, brushing her fingers over the cardboard, her eyes wet.

We ate. I liked the panettone and the custard but left all the chunks of candied fruit. Then came the clementines, one each, because it was Christmas. Maddalena peeled hers in a neat ribbon and laid out all the segments on her plate before eating them. She peeled mine too. "You can swallow the seeds too, you know. It's not true that they'll grow into a plant in your belly." Then she added, whispering in my ear, "These are not as good as the other ones." She meant Tresoldi's clementines, the only two we'd made away with the night of the test of true courage, scoffed in a hurry as we fled. Neither of us had ever brought it up again. When there were no segments left, Maddalena began sucking and chewing on the peel, grimacing.

"Here. I'm full," I said, offering her half of my clementine.

She thanked me and popped it into her mouth whole, swallowing hard, then scooped up the chunks of candied fruit I'd discarded and licked the tips of her fingers, now coated in sugar: "Can't believe how much you waste!"

"They always end too soon," Donatella commented, fingering what was left of her clementine.

"What does?" I blurted out.

Maddalena squeezed a chunk of peel near my face, squirting juice in my eyes.

"Hey!" I protested, and she laughed.

"Good things," Donatella answered, her gaze still on her hands. "They never last long enough." She blinked, and her voice faltered. "Before you know it, they're gone and all that's left is the taste."

"Are you . . . crying?" Luigia asked.

"Well, that's dumb—crying over a clementine, are you?" quipped her mother, who had just finished wiping the custard bowl clean with a finger.

"Come here, you!" Luigia leaned in and hugged Donatella, who was wiping crumbs from the table without saying a word.

Mrs. Merlini gathered the clementine peel and tossed it in the stove—"So the whole house will smell of it," she said.

Maddalena pointed at the window. "Gosh, it's really coming down now!" She jumped down from the chair, barefoot on the floor, and rushed to open the French window, stepping out onto the balcony in her flimsy blouse. Outside, snowflakes were coming down large and thick, silhouetted against the black sky.

"Shut that window, you're letting the cold in!" ordered Mrs. Merlini as she pulled her shawl tighter around her shoulders. The curtains billowed in the wind, the metal pole rattling against the furniture as snow melted on the kitchen tiles.

I joined Maddalena on the balcony to look at the flakes, which she tried to catch with her palms stretched up, tongue thrust out. "Tastes good!" She laughed.

"There's so much already. It's going to stick," I commented, pointing at the street where the light from the lampposts was being swallowed by a flurry of snowflakes, fuzzy as cotton wool. I burst out laughing. "I didn't know you could eat snow."

"Try it!" she urged me, then thrust her tongue out again, chasing the flakes with her mouth open, snatching them midair.

"Come back inside, you loonies! You'll catch your death!" Luigia shouted from the kitchen.

"Have you seen how it's coming down? It's so beautiful," Maddalena said. "And you can't hear a thing." Her bare feet were now purple, but she didn't seem to care.

Luigia covered her head with a shawl and joined us. "It's blasted cold out here." She took a breath. "Feels like we're the only people in the world." Snow fell on her hair and on her long, black lashes. "Ernesto would have loved this."

Maddalena told me it was snowing the day her parents got married too. It was so cold that her mother had given her father

her veil to wear as a scarf. Also, before the ceremony he'd apparently scalded his tongue with soup (which he'd made in the hope of warming up) and when the time came to exchange their vows before God, he could barely speak.

"Oh, for the love of God, Luigia! Shut that window!" begged Mrs. Merlini. She appeared, stopping right on the threshold of the balcony, her shadow dark and neat against the warm kitchen light. "Oh, it is beautiful though, isn't it?" She looked happy, face tilted upward, eyes closed. Then suddenly, they found Maddalena, and she looked at her. Really looked at her. She reached out to dust the snow off her hair: "Off with you now, you'll catch a fever in this cold!"

Maddalena stood completely still, stiff, mouth open yet silent, as though she'd been visited by a ghost, a memory, afraid she'd spook it away if she but took a breath. Mrs. Merlini didn't seek her daughter's eyes, didn't add anything. She went back inside and cleared the plates.

We stepped back into the comforting warmth of the kitchen, hands and cheeks purple from the cold, snowflakes melting on our skin. Maddalena scooped up chunks of snow that had settled behind my neck with shaking fingers that smelled of clementines. "Where's Donatella?" she asked then. Her chair was empty, her slice of panettone abandoned on the table, intact.

Maddalena went looking for her and I followed her out while Luigia and Mrs. Merlini tidied up the kitchen. On the landing, a strip of white light from the toilet door cut across the floor. We stepped closer, Maddalena approaching cautiously, as I'd seen her do when she snatched lizards from the cats by the Lambro.

The door was ajar. She gave it a gentle push and it opened without a sound.

Donatella was on her knees by the lavatory hole, bluish legs pressed against the floor, the cardboard crown from the panettone still on her head, slightly askew. She was crying. With every breath she threw a punch to her stomach, a feeble moan escaping her lips. She spat on the dirty ceramic, wiped her mouth with the back of her hand, and continued punching her lower belly, over and over, as if following some bizarre rhythm.

"What's got into you?" Maddalena asked.

Donatella spun around, her face a mask of anguish and horror. "Nothing. It's nothing," she blurted out, rising to her feet and smoothing the pleats of her skirt.

"You were crying."

"Crying!" she snorted, plastering on a smile. "It's just a bit of nausea. Something didn't agree with me. It's this blasted cold . . ." she said as she clumsily tidied her hair. The curl on her cheek had gone limp, heavy with sweat. The cardboard crown fell onto the floor and she didn't pick it up, squeezing past us and hurrying back to the apartment.

Maddalena and I stood looking at each other by the toilet door, as if either of us held the answers we sought. "You saw it too, didn't you?" she asked.

I nodded, but I couldn't speak. I felt we'd intruded on a secret, something dirty and mysterious, too big for us. Something that would only spell disaster.

I came home to find the lights on, my father sitting on the armchair in the hallway, and my mother, still in her finery, slumped on the kitchen table, fingers tangled in her hair, a bottle of digestif in front of her. She sprung to her feet. "How could you do something like that? Wretched girl!" she shouted.

The downstairs neighbors began pounding the ceiling with a broomstick, yelling to stop the racket already. My father stood, running his palms down his thighs as if to wipe something off, and said,

"All that matters is that she is all right. Let's go to bed, it's late. We'll discuss everything tomorrow." He locked the front door and slid the key into his dressing-gown pocket, then made for his bedroom.

"It appears your father intends to wash his hands of this, as per usual," sniped my mother. She knocked back the liqueur that still sat in her glass, then continued: "But you won't get away with it this time around, Missy. From now on, you won't leave the house unless I say so. And I'll be paying close attention, fear not."

"I'm sorry," I ventured, fear rising up in my throat at her threat. If she followed through with it, I wouldn't be able to see Maddalena.

"Do you have any idea how you embarrassed us? They asked about you after the service! Mrs. Colombo came, and the priest himself! People were staring at us. Where have you been?"

"I was at Maddalena's," I blurted out.

"I beg your pardon?" she yelled.

I looked her in the eye. "I went to the Cursed One's. We ate panettone. It was nice."

Mom laughed, and it scared me. "Well, I hope you said your goodbyes. Because you'll never see her again."

I could hear my parents arguing behind their bedroom door. It went on for some time. Lying on my bed, still fully clothed, I followed the intricate patterns of shadows chasing each other on the ceiling, thinking of how the snow had melted on my tongue, of Maddalena chewing clementine peel, of her sister's tears as she pummeled her stomach. And I felt like praying, felt like asking the Lord: "Protect them all, please."

I spent the Christmas holidays at home. My parents often dined out with the Colombos or other "notable people," but they never brought me along. I was home on New Year's Eve too, playing board games with Carla, specifically Around East Africa in Forty-Eight Stops.

"I'm so sorry, wee lamb," she said. "Might as well pack my things if I let you out this time."

The absolute worst, however, was that I had no way of warning Maddalena. What if she thought I'd abandoned her again? What if she wanted nothing to do with me anymore? Devastated, I begged and groveled, promising I wouldn't ever ask for anything else, not even for my birthday, if only they'd let me out for one hour. If they'd at least let me write to her. But it was all for nothing.

Then one day, it must have been January 5, the eve of the Epiphany (the "poor man's Christmas," when the less fortunate would receive gifts from the duce), I was sitting at the living room table concentrating on my math homework ("If ten Piccole Italiane buy half a kilo of biscuits each, for the cost of 2.25 lira . . ."). The bell rang and Carla made for the door, saying, "It must be the greengrocer's boy."

I froze, then ran after her, almost knocking the inkpot over my notebook. Noè Tresoldi's curls were limp and moist, his chin buried behind a scarf. He lifted a crate of fruit and vegetables: "Delivery for Mrs. Strada."

"You can give it to me," said Carla. "How much is it?"

"Hi," I said, my breath coming out in little bursts.

"Hi," he answered. Then to Carla: "Twenty lira and sixty cents, ma'am."

"Ooh, did you hear that? 'Ma'am' he calls me!" she teased him in a friendly tone.

I realized I was still in my nightshirt and quickly tightened the belt of my wool dressing gown, covering my chest: "I need to tell you something," I warned him.

"Me too."

Carla looked at me, then him. She grabbed the crate from his arms. "I'll just take this to the kitchen, be right back with the money. Might take me a while to get the exact change." And she disappeared, singing to herself.

Noè narrowed his eyes and stared at me.

"You have to tell Maddalena that I've been grounded. That's why I couldn't go to her. Will you tell her?"

He rubbed his hands together, blew on them. "All right."

"I thought maybe she'd come looking for me, but she didn't. Not once. Maybe she thinks I don't want to see her anymore or I've forgotten her. But that's not true, not at all! Will you tell her, please?"

"She didn't come looking for you because of what happened," he said, toying with his scarf. He sniffed: "You haven't heard, have you?"

"Heard about what?"

"That's what I wanted to tell you. The other day her sister jumped into the Lambro."

"You knew. You knew and you didn't tell me!" I'd never spoken to my parents like that before, I'd never dared. But thinking about the Cursed One stoked a fire inside me.

"These are not things one discusses with children," my mother answered calmly, sipping her hibiscus tea, saucer in one hand, cup in the other, straight out of an illustration from a good deportment book. "And it is not polite to talk about other people's misfortunes."

Dad was still buried behind his *Corriere della Sera*. Mom gave a little discreet cough. He lowered his paper, licked his lips, hesitated.

"Francesca . . ."

"I want to go to her."

"What?" My mother smacked the cup on the saucer, then spun

around to face my father. "Did you hear her? Who do you think she learned to be so impertinent from?"

"I want to see Maddalena."

Carla was in the kitchen. I could hear cups clattering in the sink.

"That is out of the question," my mother ground out. "I told you: you'll never see that girl again."

On New Year's Eve Donatella had jumped off Leoni bridge, and you could have recited a whole rosary in the time it took them to drag her out. She'd emerged black with mud, skin and lips the darkest shade of purple, clothes soaked, eyes vacant, trembling like a newborn kitten. She hadn't uttered a single word since, not even to the priest who'd stopped by. Maddalena had kicked him out, saying that priests were for the dying, and Donatella wasn't dying. She remained in bed though, covers pulled up to her chin, running a high temperature, shivering, covered in sweat.

I wasn't allowed out until school was back on January 9, since the 8th was Queen Elena's birthday and therefore still a national holiday. When my mother told me to pray for her good health, I wished she'd die for keeping me away from Maddalena another day. The following morning I rushed out before 7 a.m. and ran to Via Marsala, barely stopping to catch my breath. My throat burned as I gulped in mouthfuls of cold air that sliced through my lungs like steel. My hips, my calves throbbed with pain.

Maddalena opened the door. She was barefoot despite the cold, a light blouse peeking out of her skirt. Her eyes were so tired they seemed to have retreated far into their sockets. "Hi," she said.

"I was grounded."

"I know."

"I couldn't come to you."

"I know."

"But I wanted to. So much."

"Noè told me," she answered, stepping aside. "Want to come in?"

I dropped my schoolbag by the front door and followed her inside.

The house smelled like a bedroom that had been slept in too long, a dusky, suffocating drowsiness hanging in the air. The lights were off.

"How is your sister?"

"See for yourself."

Her mother sat by Donatella's bed, rosary beads sliding through her fingers, a wet prayer on her lips. Luigia sewed lace trimming onto a tulle veil by candlelight. Donatella's skin looked jaundiced, her limp black hair splayed across the pillow like rotting seaweed.

Maddalena grabbed my hand and led me to the kitchen. We sat at the table and I had some time to study her before she spoke. She looked thinner, all sharp edges, her face bony as well, as if she'd aged years in a few days.

"She only told me that she didn't do it because she wanted to die. She did it because she wanted to live, she said. Live at all costs. What do you think she meant?"

"I don't know." Seeing Maddalena like that hurt too much. I wished I could take it, take all her pain on me.

"She refuses to say anything else. I can't make her," she continued. When she raised her head again, she was wearing that deadly expression of hers. "Someone hurt her. I'm sure of it."

"What can we do?"

The Cursed One bit her lip until it turned white, then said, "We must find a goose and chop off its tongue."

Part IV

The
SEVERED
TONGUE
of a
GOOSE

21.

We were on the pavement opposite Tresoldi's shop, leaning against the shutters of the freshly repainted tobacconist's. Thick shadows enveloped us. In the light from the streetlamps, I could see our breaths condense in puffs of steam, which I captured with my hands for warmth.

"And what are we supposed to do with a goose?" asked Matteo, scratching his nose.

"With the tongue, not the whole goose," Maddalena corrected him.

"And what do you need a goose tongue for?" Filippo piled on.

"I'll put it under Donatella's pillow, and then she'll have to tell me the truth." Maddalena shrugged. "That's how it works."

"And how are you going to chop it off?" I inquired, a shiver running through my body.

She pulled out a knife she'd pilfered from her kitchen. "Easy," she said. "With this."

"Do you know how to use it?" Matteo cleared his throat and spat a blob of phlegm on what was left of the grayish snow on the ground.

"Want me to show you?" Maddalena goaded him, the blade glinting under the streetlamp.

Matteo raised his arms in surrender. "All right, I believe you. I believe you."

Maddalena put away the knife and pulled back a lock of hair that had flopped over her eyes. "Ready?"

I noticed the bottom of one of her pockets was heavy and sodden, giving off a foul smell.

"What else have you got in there?"

"You'll see."

"Ready!" Matteo banged a fist on the palm of his other hand.

"We're going to get into trouble . . ." Filippo whined.

Maddalena darted to the pavement opposite us but didn't stop at the greengrocer's shutters. Instead, she ran toward the large door that opened onto the building's inner courtyard.

"Now what?" I asked as soon as I was next to her.

"We're going in."

"How?"

"How do you usually get into a building?"

"You need a key. And we don't have one."

The Cursed One smiled, then she turned and held out her hand to Matteo, who began rummaging in his coat. He dug out a scuffed old key and hesitated before dropping it in her palm.

"Where did you get that?"

"Are you stupid or what?" asked Matteo with a loud snort.

Offended, I screwed up my lips and bit back: "Why would you keep a key now the butcher shop's gone?"

"Because I knew I'd be back one day."

"If we have a key, then it's not stealing, right?" asked Filippo from behind his back, eyes wide as saucers.

"Shut up, all of you. They'll hear us!" hissed the Cursed One, slotting the key into the lock. She turned it twice and the lock disengaged. With both palms resting on the dark wood, she pushed, then waved at us to hurry inside as she held the door open. Matteo and Filippo obeyed, soon disappearing into the darkness.

Maddalena and I were alone. She turned to face me and held out her hand. "Are you coming in?"

"Do you really believe that?" I asked, her hand suspended between us, waiting for me to take it. "That thing about the tongue, I mean."

The Cursed One looked at me as if I were a child. "Of course I do. Don't you?"

I laced my fingers through hers. "If you believe it, then I believe it too."

The entrance corridor was dark, a soapy smell lingering in the air as we walked past the empty station, silent as a church. We reached the courtyard, fear knotting our throats, naked, cold-hardened ground under our shoes. Filippo and Matteo froze, shoulders flattening against the wall, and looked around. The Cursed One kept going and gestured at us to follow her.

"No," Matteo grimaced, courage coming back to him. "I used to live here. I'm the one who knows the way."

Maddalena stared at him, then stepped aside.

Matteo walked past me, deliberately shouldering me out of the way, and kept going until he reached the dimly lit courtyard, where old furniture and splintered pallets were stacked in a corner. "This is it," he said, pointing at a black gate topped with barbed wire that separated Tresoldi's property from the rest of the courtyard.

That's when the dog started barking. We jumped back, and I stifled a scream. Glinting orange eyes, dirty foam dripping from his mouth, white fangs like jagged bones, the dog thrust his muzzle through the bars as his claws scraped the dirt.

Matteo tore a length of wood from a broken crate. "I'm going to kill him."

"Stand back," said the Cursed One, jabbing her elbow into Matteo's side.

He coughed.

From her dripping pocket she extracted something flabby and red, dark juices flowing down her sleeve.

"What's that now?" asked Filippo, pinching his nose.

Maddalena stepped toward the gate as the dog twisted his head, growling, muzzle squashed between the bars, drool oozing out in fat drops.

"Do you want this?" she taunted him, dangling the meat over his nose.

"He's going to bite your hand off!"

"Careful!"

"Come on, let's get back." I tugged at the hem of her coat but she broke free. She was so close now that the dog could have bitten the nose off her face. We heard him suck his breath in, then he started panting, sniffing the meat, a low growl still rumbling in his throat. As he threw his jaws open to snatch the treat, Maddalena jerked her arm up, stretched it behind her back, and lobbed the meat over the gate. It smacked against the wall and landed in the dust. Jumping away from the bars, the dog darted toward the back of Tresoldi's yard.

My bones ached. It was only then that I realized my teeth had been clattering the whole time.

"Come on, before he gobbles it up!" urged Maddalena.

"And how do we get to the other side?" Filippo pointed at the barbed wire.

"We climb over it."

"If we get sliced on that, we won't live to tell the tale, that's for sure," Matteo cut in, tapping the piece of wood on his shoulder.

"How about using that?" I replied, pointing at a dirty, frayed blanket abandoned on the wooden crates. "We could throw it on the barbed wire so we can climb over it."

The Cursed One smiled. "Nice one." The rosettes they gave us at school, the compliments from the grown-ups—they all seemed stupid and insignificant next to one of her smiles.

Matteo and Filippo folded the blanket twice so it wouldn't shred on the barbed wire and tossed it over the gate on the count of three. Maddalena went first. With her feet lodged between the bars, she sank her arms into the blanket for leverage and jumped. "It worked!" she whispered, landing in the backyard where Tresoldi kept his animals.

Matteo was next, then he helped Filippo over the gate. I tried to climb too, but I wasn't strong enough. Maddalena stared at me but didn't move. She wanted to see if I could make it by myself. Was this another test? I set my jaw the way I'd seen her do, bent my knees, and jumped. For a moment, there was nothing. Then came the ground, brutal and hard against my shoulder, my hip, my elbow. A sharp whine escaped my lips. My body was on fire. Matteo laughed. "Ssshhh," said the Cursed One, a finger pressed against her lips. She pulled me up. "You're all right. It's nothing," she commented, checking the spots where my coat had torn.

"It's nothing," I repeated, wiping the dust off my face.

"C'mon, you lazy ass. We've got to hurry," said Matteo.

The dog licked at the bone lodged between his paws, the meat chewed clean off it.

We moved forward in the semidarkness teeming with shadows. Chickens in wooden coops, hay bales, dirty tools propped up against a chipped wall, broken crates, a trough filled with foul-smelling water, and over it all, the stench of what my father called *"buascia"* when we went hiking in the mountains or on the bridle paths along the fields. "Watch out, don't step on that!" he'd say, pointing at the cowpats, flat and round like potlids. It was as if Tresoldi had cut off a chunk of countryside and transplanted it into his backyard.

The geese were inside their pen, a pallet resting sideways against the low fence to serve as a ladder, a sheet of corrugated iron as roof. They slept on the damp hay, necks rounded, beaks buried in their feathers.

"We need to pick one," said the Cursed One.

"And then what?" asked Matteo.

"Then we kill it."

"Do you know how?"

"No." The Cursed One shrugged. "But people do it every day. How hard can it be?"

She threw a leg over the pen. "Are you coming or what?"

The silence weighed on me. When I joined her, she was squatting next to the sleeping geese, feathers quivering in the icy breeze. "They're so beautiful," I said.

"And fat," she added, wielding the knife. "Tresoldi stuffs food down their necks to make liver pâté."

She hesitated, watching the geese sleep, knife in her hand and breath coming in short pants out of her open mouth.

"Are you sure you want to do this?"

"I have to get the tongue," she answered, swallowing hard, eyes glinting in the dark. "There's no other way."

"Do you want us to hold it down?" Matteo suggested.

"What if it starts honking?" asked Filippo.

"We'll kill it before it gets the chance."

"So you, what, wring its neck like a chicken?" Filippo countered.

A sudden howl pierced the silence.

Matteo cursed, Filippo dropped his head in his hands. "Oh God, we're going to get caught!"

The dog started whining, scratched at the ground as if in a frenzy, whined again—a powerful, pained whimper.

The Cursed One grimaced. "I'll go check. Wait here," she said, handing the knife to Matteo.

She jumped clear out of the pen and the darkness swallowed her, the hem of her oversize coat flapping against her bare thighs, which gleamed white in the cold moonlight.

I turned. Matteo and Filippo were staring at me. A knowing glance passed between them, they nodded.

"Come on, we have to do it now. Quick!" Filippo whispered behind Matteo, who gripped the knife in his hand.

"What are you looking at?"

"We've decided you have to go," Matteo said.

"Who's decided?"

"Us."

"Us who?"

"Us three."

"That's not true."

"Yes it is!" Filippo bit back.

"You can't be with us. We don't want you."

"I made a mistake that time at school. But I passed the clementine test. She's forgiven me."

"I don't care if she's forgiven you. We don't want you," Matteo said. "You want to steal her away from us."

"You've already stolen her away!" Filippo interjected in a shrill voice.

"That's not true!" I protested.

"So what were you doing at hers?"

"She's never let us into her house."

"What have you got that we don't, huh?"

"You've got to go!" hissed Filippo, gripping Matteo's shoulder, tongue darting through the gap in his teeth. "Or I swear we'll kill you!"

"No," I said, my chest heaving with icy, labored breaths.

"Then you better start running."

My legs quivered. "I don't want to leave Maddalena. Not for anything in the world."

"She doesn't want people to use her name."

"She lets me use it."

Matteo's lips twisted in a horrifying grimace. "You make me sick!"

He was lightning fast: his arm darted forward and was back at his side before I even felt the pain. But there was blood on the blade now, dripping on the cold-hardened ground.

I lifted one hand to my cheek, where a gash burned already.

"Check if she's coming back!" said Matteo, his eyes trained on me.

Filippo nodded, leaning on the fence. "Not yet."

The dog kept howling at the back of the yard.

"We've got time then." Matteo ran his tongue over his lips. "Look, I don't want to hurt a girl," he continued. "Just go away, all right?"

Blood oozed thick and warm through my fingers, and suddenly my knees buckled. Tears flooded my eyes, turning everything into a blur.

Matteo, meanwhile, threatened me: "And if you tell the Cursed One, I'll chop off your tongue too. Like a goose!"

I started sobbing.

It wasn't him I was afraid of, or that knife he didn't know how to use. But I couldn't explain how I got that cut on my face to my parents. I'd managed to steal the house keys from Mom's handbag, which she'd left on the sideboard by the main door, and sneak out without making a sound. But what would I tell her in the morning, with my face in such a state? There was no way I could hide it. It was proof I was up to something.

Matteo was laughing out loud. "Women cry more than dogs piss!" he snarled, one of his father's sayings again. "Now go away. Leave us alone. And stop whining!"

I scooped up a handful of dirt and hurled it at him. He staggered back, trying to wipe his eyes with the sleeve of his coat. "I'm not afraid of you!" I shouted. The geese began honking all at once in a whirlwind of wings, dust, and hay. I hopped sideways to put some distance between us, and that's when Filippo, hearing the commotion, rejoined us. He tackled me and pinned me to the ground. Matteo grabbed my ankle. "I'll chop off your tongue . . ."

Filippo clamped a hand over my mouth and I bit his fingers. He let out a piercing cry, then slapped me.

"What are you doing?" Suddenly the Cursed One appeared.

Lights started flickering on in the windows and balconies around us.

"What are you doing?" repeated Maddalena in a voice I'd never heard her use before.

"She got frightened and wanted to call the grown-ups," Matteo replied, his breaths uneven.

"We had to stop her." Filippo added.

I couldn't speak, couldn't stop crying, one of my hands pressed hard against my cheek, where blood still flowed.

The Cursed One stood, legs apart, feet firmly planted on the ground, eyes wide open. She stared at Matteo and Filippo, looking like the bronze statue of the war memorial, the one wielding a sword, a war cry forever etched on her face. "Go away," she said.

"No, w-wait," Matteo stammered. "It was her! It was all her fault!"

"You shouldn't have let her come to the river with us. You shouldn't have!" Filippo added.

Maddalena didn't even blink anymore, her face hard, pale, perfectly still. "You're afraid now. You feel like you're about to die. Something bad's going to happen to you now."

Filippo covered his ears and started whining. "I didn't want to do it!" he protested. "It was him. I didn't want to!"

"You're going to get hurt. Maybe you'll fall and your bones will stick out of your knees. Maybe the river rats will chew off your toes. Or maybe, when you climb the fence again, the barbed wire will sink into your gut."

She started toward Matteo.

He stepped back. "She's just a stupid little girl. I've done it for you, can't you see?"

"You're a jealous little boy." Maddalena kept walking toward him.

Matteo stepped sideways. A cry. A shrill, bloodcurdling cry. He fell to the ground, doubled over, arms wrapped around one of his legs, rolling around in the dirt surrounded by honking geese. There was a nail sticking out of the sole of his foot, blood gushing out in all directions.

Maddalena bent over me. "Are you all right?"

I nodded, sniffing, and wiped my face with my sleeve. I grabbed her hand and pulled myself up. She hugged me and I shook in her arms while Matteo kept rolling and shrieking.

Filippo was nowhere to be seen, he'd already bolted.

Voices from the windows and balconies: "Who's there? Thieves! Someone go and have a look!"

"We have to run!" I said.

"We can't leave Matteo here like this," the Cursed One answered. "And I still need my tongue."

"But what if someone comes?"

"We're not afraid of anyone. Never forget this. Anyone."

Now the lights were all on and the yard looked like the nativity scene they set up in the cathedral every year. Curious women wrapped in shawls peeked out from windows and balconies, their hair tucked into nets. A rumble of steps on the staircase as men approached fast, faster.

The gate was flung open with such force that it clattered against the wall, and in no time a gaggle of men in dressing gowns and slippers made for us, the dog wagging his tail and jumping around their leader, who held a torch in one hand and a rifle in the other.

"What the hell are you doing here?" he said, his face now visible, lit by the torch. On it, the same mean look I'd witnessed every time he'd discovered us. He stepped over the low fence and came so close I could smell the warmth of his bed on him, and over it garlic and sweat.

I was certain I was going to die. Tresoldi would wring our necks like he did with his chickens. Maddalena squared up to him and looked him straight in the eye. "We wanted to steal a goose," she said, perfectly serious. "Then he got hurt." She pointed at Matteo, who was whimpering like a puppy. "So we didn't manage to steal anything."

Tresoldi burst out laughing. "They're right to call you the Cursed One, so they are."

Maddalena still held my hand behind her back. Only I could feel her shake. "This was all my idea," she continued. "They just came along. But I need the goose, for real, and I'm not leaving without one."

A beastly laugh rumbled up Tresoldi's throat. The other men muttered but remained outside the fence, huddling like a flock of pigeons eyeing a weasel.

"Nice mess you've made," said Tresoldi. "What am I supposed to do with you now, huh?" Maddalena's eyes were still trained on his. Tresoldi propped the rifle against the fence and shooed the geese away with his foot, then walked toward Matteo and lifted him like a knobbly sack of clementines.

"Get back to bed," he said to the other men. "I'll handle this."

Some protested, some remained quiet. But nobody moved, and nobody made to leave.

"I said get back to bed!" repeated Tresoldi. He pointed the torch at the women leaning on their balconies. "You too, back to bed. This is my backyard, and you'll do as I say." Then he spun back and heaved a semiconscious Matteo over his shoulder, blood dripping all over his dirty dressing gown. "You," he said, looking at us. "Come with me."

Tresoldi's kitchen was bathed in the cold light of a bare light bulb hanging from the ceiling. The bulb swung in the breeze that blew in from the window, which had been left ajar, painting large shadows over our faces and across the copper pots hooked to the blackened wall by the stove. Noè stood up to close the window, then slumped back onto his chair, a resigned look on his face. "You're crazy."

Matteo lay on the sofa, bandaged foot sunk into a cushion, a frayed crochet coverlet on his shoulders. Tears and snot had dried in clumps under his nose and on his cheeks. He wouldn't look at anyone and was yet to say a word since the accident.

"It's nothing serious," Tresoldi had reassured him as he applied iodine tincture to the wound. "You're lucky you've still got your toes. The nail was new, so no need to worry about infections. All that blood makes it look far worse than it is."

"Keep an eye on them," he'd said to Noè as he headed back to the yard. "I'll check on the geese."

Noè's eyelids were heavy with sleep, his curls flattened on one side. Maddalena kept scratching grooves on the tablecloth, then smoothing them over with her palm. The silence in that kitchen crushed me. I ran my fingers over the dried blood on my cheek, and despite the fear, despite the pain that had begun to dull, that wound made me feel important.

"Does it hurt?" asked Noè.

"This?" I asked. "It's nothing."

A hint of a smile ghosted across Maddalena's lips, her eyes still on the tablecloth.

"What were you thinking?" Noè ventured, but Maddalena kept dragging her nails across the tablecloth without a word. He rocked back on his chair and reached for an old Bible lying on one corner of the mantelpiece, then slapped it on the table, extracting a packet of tobacco from his pocket. In a series of slow, measured movements, Noè opened the Bible, ripped off a tissue-thin page, sprinkled a pinch of tobacco on it and started shaping it into a cylinder, wetting one side with his saliva.

"I need to get that tongue," Maddalena said as Noè lit a match against the stone fireplace.

"The tongue?" he asked, exhaling smoke. "And what do you need it for?"

"It makes people tell the truth. It's for Donatella," she answered. "I need to know who hurt her."

At that moment, Tresoldi came back from the yard, slamming the door against the mantelpiece. He dumped something heavy and white on the kitchen table and the light bulb oscillated wildly, sending crazy patterns of light and shadows crashing around the room. "The feathers have to be plucked the way they grow—in this direction, all right? Start at the tail, then all the way up to the neck. That clear?"

In a flash, Maddalena pulled her hands back from the table and nodded, a serious look on her face. The dead goose's feet were tied together, its beak wide open, tongue dangling out, wings spread over the oilcloth. There was a crack in its skull, caked in blood, as though someone had punched a hole through it from inside its mouth.

"Then you have to gut it. Better ask someone who's done it before. The organs need to come out, but don't chuck 'em, you hear me? The liver's a delicacy. Do you like liver?"

"Of course," Maddalena said. "Of course I like it."

"Good." Tresoldi nodded and wiped his fingers on his shapeless pants. He looked at her, then me. "Her name was Elena. Like the queen."

"Who?"

"The goose. I name every single one of them. And I don't forget. When you kill one, you have to say a prayer and send her off to meet the Lord."

"Why? Do geese have a soul too?"

"You bet they do." Tresoldi was dead serious. "All creatures have a soul."

"And you're giving this goose to me?" asked Maddalena. "Even though I wanted to steal her? And you said you'd feed *us* to the geese? And you know we took the cherries?"

Tresoldi took a long breath, pulled out a chair next to his son, and dropped on it with a muffled grunt. "Make me one," he said, pointing at the Bible.

While Noè rolled the cigarette, Tresoldi kept his gaze trained on Maddalena. His eyes were small, hidden almost, in the yellow folds of his skin. "I heard about your siblings," he said. "Nasty business. One packed off to war in Africa, the other jumping in the river . . ." He lit the cigarette and began puffing greedily, as if he wanted to swallow it. "Stealing is wrong," he continued, "but you girls have got more guts than most soldiers out there." He stared at me too, and I wished I could disappear.

"Maddalena only did it because she had to, Sir," I said, breath catching in my throat. "Please don't punch a hole through our skull with the scissors like you did with the goose, I'm begging you."

"Well, well. She speaks!" said Tresoldi, his laugh loud as a hailstorm. He stubbed the cigarette on the sole of his boot, then added, looking at the Cursed One, "I thought you were the one who went around cracking people's skulls, you know? I believed what people said, and I always thought it too, not gonna lie. But the truth is that you burrow into people's heads and never leave. That's what you do."

22.

It was Noè who put the severed goose tongue under Donatella's pillow. He did it in the dead of night, the stench of fever saturating the house. Gentle as a mother would be, he lifted a corner of the pillow and slid the fist-sized bundle containing the severed tongue, wet and red, underneath.

"Don't wake her," Maddalena whispered from the opposite side of the bed.

Donatella's head thrashed this way and that. She whined like dogs do when they dream, grinding her teeth, sweat dripping down her face.

"Now what?" I asked, gripping the brass bars at the bottom of the bed.

"Now we wait." Maddalena smoothed a damp lock of hair off her sister's sweaty forehead.

Next to the bed, I saw the two chairs where Luigia and Mrs. Merlini sat during the day, a Bible and rosary beads abandoned there next to the unfinished veil, a pair of scissors, and a spool of white thread.

Maddalena bent over her sister's face and asked, "Who hurt you?"

We held our breath, perfectly quiet. Then, her eyes two narrow slits, Donatella answered: "The baby."

"The baby?" Maddalena prodded. "Whose baby?"

"Mine," she blurted. "Mine and Tiziano's baby."

23.

I t was on a bright, bitterly cold January afternoon that Maddalena and I tracked down Tiziano Colombo.

He was sitting at one of the tables outside the café on Piazza dell'Arengario, which my mother called the "chic café" because the waiters wore a bow tie and white gloves and served pastries on little silver trays. She liked going there after mass in the spring, to eat ice cream out of pewter cups, listen to the string quartet, and bask in the envy of passersby. Most of the tables were empty because of the cold, except for those occupied by Tiziano, a few other men, and an elegant young lady in a fur muff and coral earrings. The men were young and handsome, all pressed uniforms and carefully coiffed hair. Tiziano laughed as he sipped his hot chocolate, wrapped in a heavy black coat.

"You!" shouted Maddalena, staring at him from across the red velvet rope that enclosed the tables. I stood next to her, breathing through my nose to hide my fear.

"Are they talking to you?" asked one of the boys, lanky and awkward.

Tiziano saw us and waved us closer, looking perfectly at ease. Maddalena didn't hesitate. She threw a leg over the rope and in no time she was right in front of him. I followed her without saying a word, looking on as she wrung her hands so hard the cracked skin over her knuckles started bleeding again. "I know why you stopped coming to see my sister," she blurted.

"I'm sorry, but these are not things one discusses with children," Tiziano answered.

"What does this poor wretch want with you?" the lady asked, leaning over Tiziano's shoulder. "Good Lord, she's dirty!"

"You turning little girls' heads too now?" joked a dark-haired, clean-faced guy, looking at us with such intensity my cheeks flushed.

"I'm not in the mood to talk about your sister," Tiziano reprised, a sad look on his face. "It's all in the past anyway."

The night the severed goose tongue made Donatella confess the truth, I'd remembered hearing Tiziano say he was going to marry her. Now I knew the Cursed One was right—although he was handsome, he was not to be trusted.

"Her name is Donatella Merlini. She's your girlfriend. She jumped in the Lambro for you. And now you want to cast her off, like an old pair of shoes?" Maddalena didn't waver. Her voice was loud and clear, like the men who talked about war on the radio.

"Enough with these miserable memories," interjected another from behind his round glasses as he sipped his barley water. "His poor heart can't handle it."

"His poor heart, huh?" hissed Maddalena. "That'd be the same heart that keeps him here drinking hot chocolate instead of going to war? His *sick* heart?"

Tiziano's hand jerked as if he was swatting away a fly.

"I thought she was a good girl, I was very fond of her," he said with a pained expression. "That was before I learned the truth."

"Liar!" hissed Maddalena.

"I'm sorry, but that's just how things are. I should have

known . . . that lipstick she wore . . . she wanted men's attention, it was clear."

The lady with the fur muff curled her lips in a disdainful grimace. "Shameful!"

"Your sister had other men. The proof's in that swelling belly of hers."

"That's your baby and you know it!" Maddalena shouted, and everyone went quiet. "She wanted to drown it in the Lambro but she didn't manage to. What d'you think she'll do now, huh?"

Tiziano huffed, scornful.

"That's what happens in families where there's no father figure," said a man in thick woolen gloves.

"Women are like a lit fireplace in winter: as soon as smoke puffs out of the chimney, the blackbirds start circling!" joked the dark-haired one. The men laughed.

Maddalena's eyes were glued to the ground now, her shoulders shaking.

"That's not true!" I said, swallowing my fear and shame. "You're all liars."

"You do see that a Colombo couldn't possibly get involved with a . . . swallow," commented another.

"What's a swallow?" the Cursed One asked.

"A cheap girl," said the young lady. "One that flutters into some rented apartment with a gentleman and emerges with ruffled feathers come sundown."

"That's not true!"

"And they say men have filthy minds!"

Tiziano raised a hand as if to stop the comments, then turned to face Maddalena: "Do be kind. You wouldn't want a certain rumor to spread, would you? It would pain me to see Mrs. Merlini even more heartbroken—she has enough worries as it is. Why would you go and pile more on?"

"Nasty business," said the dark-haired one, raking a hand through his pomaded locks.

"Such an unlucky family . . ." commented the girl as she fidgeted with one of her earrings, lost in thought.

Tiziano extracted a wad of cash in a silver clip from his pocket, licked the tip of his index finger, then pulled out a brown note the size of a pillowcase. I'd never seen a thousand lira up close before. He folded it in half and slid it across the table toward Maddalena: "Take it."

"How very charitable!" commented the girl, brushing Tiziano's hand. He shrugged as if that money was nothing to him.

"We cannot abandon those in need. Not even in cases such as this."

"The girl had it coming though."

"Such a big heart, Tiziano. Such a big heart."

When Maddalena looked up, her face was strained, tears wetting her lashes. She inhaled sharply and spat at Tiziano, his eyes wide as saucers as a blob of saliva dripped down his coat right onto his Fascist Party pin.

"You're going to die soon," Maddalena snarled, staring right into his black pupils. "I swear to you. You'll die like a swollen river rat, with crows picking at your guts."

The smile faded from Tiziano's face at the Cursed One's words. His confidence seemed to falter for a moment, then his laughter joined the others', loud and booming.

Maddalena didn't utter a single word on the way back from the café. She walked ahead of me at a brisk pace and ignored me even when I called her name, the too-big coat flapping around her like wings as she marched down Via Vittorio Emanuele. I followed her, my breathing choppy and uneven. I thought about Donatella, her painted lips and tight dresses, and that word came swirling around my head again: *swallow*. I hated Tiziano, his measured, knowing words, but nowhere near as much as I hated myself: for a moment, only a moment, I'd believed him.

We found Noè in his backyard, digging a hole behind the goose pen. He smiled when he saw us and waved, then he noticed Maddalena was furious and kept digging. The dog pulled at his chain and barked madly, covering the rhythmic pounding of Noè's shovel against the ice-hardened soil.

Without stopping, Noè looked at me and said, "It's healed."

My hand flew to my cheek, where Matteo had slashed me with Maddalena's knife the night we'd snuck into that very same backyard. Face wounds always bleed a lot, even surface wounds, he'd explained. Mine was just a scratch.

My mother had seen it when it was still fresh: "How did you get that, you wretched girl?" she'd shouted. I'd answered I'd done it to myself, on purpose, to spite her, because if my future really rested on nothing but my pretty face, then I wanted no part of it. She'd screwed her lips, saying that if the cut left a scar, no man would want to marry me and I'd end up alone, and I'd only have myself to blame. "So be it" had been my answer. The wound had healed quickly, and I was almost sorry about it.

"Even if it had left a mark, it wouldn't matter," Noè blurted out. "You'd still be beautiful."

I felt my cheeks flush and didn't answer.

"What are you doing?" Maddalena asked him.

"Digging a hole."

"I can see that. What for?"

"I'd come out to get a goose. Then I smelled something rotten behind the crates, down there, and went to have a look."

"And what did you find?"

"Want to see for yourselves?"

The cat's eyes were white, his belly torn open. Noè swatted away the flies on his snout with the shovel. "He must have snuck in last night. Bet Vittorio toyed with him some before he let him go—and he came to die over here."

"Who's Vittorio?" I asked, covering my mouth to stop myself from retching.

"The dog. Dad called him Vittorio Emanuele—after the king."

"Oh."

Noè shrugged. "Dad said to throw him out. The cat. But I feel sorry for him."

"That's a bad omen," Maddalena cut in. "An omen of death."

"Animals die here every day. You shouldn't believe this nonsense," Noè replied.

"Don't you?" she shot back.

"Believe in bad omens and bad luck? No. These are just stories people make up because they're afraid."

"So you don't believe a goose tongue will make you tell the truth either?"

"No."

"And what they say about me? Do you believe that?"

"No."

Maddalena was silent for a few seconds, then grabbed the shovel from Noè's hands. "We'll help you."

The three of us picked up the dead cat using an old blanket so we wouldn't have to touch it, and so his guts wouldn't leak all over the yard. The carcass was so heavy it felt like it'd been stuffed with rocks, puny as it looked, black and dirty in the middle of the blanket.

I had to hold my breath until we dropped the bundle into the hole behind the goose pen.

"Why did you come here?" Noè said as he replaced the shovel in the toolshed.

"Do you know how to kill a goose?" Maddalena asked.

Noè rubbed a clump of dirt off his chin. "Yes," he replied, laconic.

"Show me how it's done, then," she said, with that look on her face—the look she got when she was plotting something evil.

"Why do you want to know?" I asked her.

Noè found a pair of long, sharp scissors. "Need another tongue?" he probed, as we walked toward the pen.

"No," Maddalena answered. "I just want to learn how to kill."

Whatever she had in mind, she didn't have time to follow through with it. The very evening we buried the cat, news came that would forever change Maddalena's family's life.

A telegram from Africa: Ernesto had been wounded during the "heroic" (that's what they called it) defense of the Uarieu Pass stronghold and transferred to a military hospital. More news would follow in the coming days, the telegram promised in its impersonal, officious voice.

Maddalena could not sleep or eat for forty-eight hours. Then Ernesto himself wrote from the hospital. He didn't mention anything about his condition or whether he might be sent back home—he only asked about Luigia. He wanted to marry her. Immediately. Before it was too late. They arranged everything via telegram, and then the last letter came. Black corners.

Luigia was bent over the kitchen table, head buried in her arms. Her glasses lay abandoned on the tablecloth, the unfinished veil still resting on her hair. Mrs. Merlini had locked herself up in her room and we could hear her wailing all the way into the kitchen. Donatella slept.

"Ernesto was afraid of dying before he could marry her," Maddalena explained, choking on her breath, wringing the letter like a dishcloth. "They did everything by proxy. She said yes from here, he said yes from Africa, and they sorted everything out."

On January 24, the Battle of Tembien had ended in neither victory nor defeat, and Ernesto, like so many others, had died in vain. I stepped closer and grabbed Maddalena's hand. She squeezed mine and lifted it to her forehead, keeping it there for a long time, saying nothing. That was the kind of pain no words could speak.

24.

I dreamed of geese for nights on end.

They were restless dreams, confused, violent. Battlefields strewn with corpses like the painting of the Napoleonic Wars in my schoolbook. The soldiers, however, didn't have rifles but long, shiny scissors like the ones Noè used to kill geese. And he was in the dream too, wearing a green helmet, arms caked in blood up to his elbows, holding the stiff carcass of a goose whose belly had been slashed open. "You have to feel your way around the guts with your hand," he explained to Maddalena, "then scrape them out with your fingers. But mind they don't burst, or the meat will taste foul."

Because Maddalena was there too, and Tiziano Colombo, with a long, crooked neck and a beak attached to that clean, handsome face of his. In the dream, Maddalena drove the scissors into his mouth and up through his skull, and he screamed as black liquid spurted from his head. Then his stomach swelled and a baby burst out, and the baby's skin was purple, like a drowned man's. Then I'd wake up, drenched in sweat and fear, wanting to scream.

I wished I could tell Maddalena about it, about my dreams, but she avoided me. After Ernesto's death she had built up a barrier around her that no one could breach. "Tomorrow," she'd answer from behind her door when I went looking for her. But the following day was no different from the one before. I learned from Carla that Donatella's fever had broken and she was no longer bedridden, but her belly kept swelling and Mrs. Merlini, overwhelmed with shame, kept her out of sight. Maddalena had chosen to hole up with them in that cold, desolate house.

Without her, everything appeared leeched of its colors, shape, texture. Our geography teacher kept pinning flags on a map of Ethiopia to mark the army's advance in what she described as "the greatest colonial venture in history." I hated her with such intensity that I fantasized about standing up and smashing the inkpot on her forehead.

Instead, I did nothing. I'd just look out the window, waiting for the bell to ring, and dart out without saying goodbye to anyone after the last class. Staying away from Maddalena cost me, so I'd sprint through the town center, schoolbag slapping my thighs, almost tripping over my undone scarf, and go see Noè.

I liked his scent—wet soil and hard work and tobacco—and his slow, measured movements, never wasted on anything that didn't need doing. He let me keep him company while he worked, and I talked to him about anything that'd help deaden the noise in my head. He listened and asked a few questions while he fed the geese or lined up tubs of preserve on the top shelves. Even Tresoldi had come to accept my presence there, the way you accept flies in summer. He'd see me in his shop, balanced on a ladder, handing a can of stock cubes to Noè, and mutter, "Haven't you got homework to do or something?"

"Already done," I'd reply, shrugging.

Sometimes, Noè asked me to repeat my lessons—he didn't want me to fail the year, he said, or I'd be bothering him in the morning too if I wasn't in school. He soon got bored, however, with stories of Ulysses climbing into the Trojan horse, or Catullus grieving his brother (*Will I never, oh brother more beloved than life itself, behold you hereafter?*)

When I went to see him, he'd rather be the one explaining how things worked, the things he knew about: how hens made eggs, where you had to tap them with your finger to know if there was a chick inside or not. The rooster, he said, should always be kept away because he never tired of getting the hens pregnant. Even when he spoke about these matters, Noè was never vulgar, and never shied away from topics that other men—such as my father or my teachers— would consider shameful and inappropriate for a girl.

The void left by the Cursed One smarted like a blister from a deep burn. I clung to Noè, cocooning myself in his affection, pretending it was enough, and for a while, the dreams went away.

Then one day, in the coop, Noè tipped my chin up. "You're beautiful, you know that?" He was so quick I didn't have time to back out: dipping his head, he pressed his lips to mine, delicate but firm, wet and hot. His tongue sought mine, which remained still. Our mingled breaths tasted odd—I didn't like it. Feeling him on me like that made my heart pump faster, but I pushed him away, frightened. "What are you doing?" I panted, shoving him.

"I'm sorry . . ." he stuttered, stepping back.

The eggs we'd been collecting lay cracked on the ground in a clear yellow blob and the hens clucked raucously, scattering white feathers streaked with dirt all over the coop.

That night, the nightmares came back. I woke up in the dark, fear lodged in my throat, sheets sticking to my skin, and remembered the only people I could confide in were no longer available to me. I tossed and turned, rubbing my face against the pillow, pretending it was Noè's shoulder or Maddalena's side.

Then I fell asleep again.

25.

Winter came to an end and I barely noticed. The balmy glow of spring slowly edged its way through the last of the cold days—it was in the cawing of crows circling the Lambro, in the buds shooting out on tree branches, round and sleek like marbles.

"What's the matter with you?" my mother asked that Sunday, March 15, as I buckled the shoes that sliced through my heels.

"Nothing," I replied, when I really wanted to say "Everything."

I crossed Leoni bridge with Dad, who walked briskly without looking back, and Mom, who followed a few steps behind, clutching her ostrich-feather bag to her side. I stopped and leaned on the parapet: the river flowed gray and silent, a flock of ducks resting on the pebbles by the shore. It was as though the Cursed Ones had never existed.

The cathedral square was bathed in sunshine, the sky completely clear. Street artists, faces smeared with chalk, pants torn at the knee, drew portraits of Mussolini and Jesus on the pavement, next to a pleading sign that read, "Spare a coin for the artist." Old ladies in black moved in tight packs toward the church—long skirts, fishnet gloves, headscarves.

My mother stopped outside the cathedral, its imposing black and white facade warmed by the sun, and plucked a veil that smelled of talcum powder from her bag. We had to move out of the way as the Colombos' black Balilla came to a halt next to us, the sound of gravel scrunching under its tires demanding people turn, step aside, admire it.

Colombo stepped out of the car. My father took off his hat, and my mother lit up, straightening her shoulders, preening and puffing her feathers like a dove.

"Mr. Strada, how nice to see you," Colombo began, a wide grin spreading across his face. Then he turned to face my mother: "Madam," he whispered, in an overly polite, oily tone that smacked of arrogance, implying he could have called her anything he wanted. He bowed to her, eyes slowly raking her figure as he straightened.

Filippo and Tiziano emerged from the back seats, both sporting a middle parting, well-pressed uniforms, and freshly polished black boots. Tiziano was helping his mother out of the car. One foot resting on the foldable steps, she leaned on the white muslin parasol she wielded like a walking cane.

"Good morning, Mrs. Colombo," my father greeted her.

"Good morning to you."

"Let's sit together," Colombo suggested, hooking his thumbs in his black belt.

"Capital idea!" replied my mother, looking at him adoringly.

"My, how your daughter has grown! A proper young lady!" Mrs. Colombo said to my father.

"That she is," he answered, with a surge of pride that surprised me. Confined in those elegant clothes—silk skirt and coat—I felt wrong, out of place. I folded my arms across my chest.

"Don't you think Francesca has grown into such a beautiful

young lady?" Mrs. Colombo pressed Filippo, placing a hand on his shoulder. He grimaced and his father's face twisted into an annoyed scowl. "Answer your mother."

Tiziano came to his aid, dipping his head: "A beautiful young lady indeed." He bowed like his father had, and as he straightened, one of his hands brushed the hem of my skirt. "And such a nice dress."

I jumped back, vexed, and shouted, "No!"

My mother was horrified. "Francesca! What manners are these?"

"I don't want him to touch me," I hissed.

"And what are you afraid of?" Colombo laughed. "He doesn't bite, you know?"

"No," I said, my eyes hard as Maddalena's would have been. "But maybe he'll put a baby in my belly and make me jump in the river."

Everyone was left speechless, the veneer of politeness gone. The first thing I felt was the smack—the full weight of my mother's hand connecting with my cheek. Then came Mrs. Colombo's words: "My family has nothing to do with that deranged woman!"

Mr. Colombo scrutinized me with a mix of disgust and disappointment. Filippo clung to his mother's skirts while Tiziano flashed me a disturbing smile.

"Utterly deranged!" repeated Mrs. Colombo, turning her back on us to walk into the church, followed by her husband and sons.

"You idiot!" my mother yelled. "Why did you have to say that?"

She chased after Mr. Colombo, calling him by his first name, holding on to her hat as she ran, all her lectures on dignity and reputation seemingly forgotten. The old ladies who walked past us pointed at my mother, whispering, "See how the swallow hurries back to her nest!"

My father put his hat back on, his gaze to the ground. Had we really been so blind all that time? Him, refusing to see, me not yet

understanding that I'd seen far too much. I walked into the church
pressing a hand to my cheek, which still smarted. Dad led me down
the aisle and I took care to only step on the *black* marble tiles, clacking my heels as I went. When we found my mother on the bench
behind the Colombos, my father sat next to her as if nothing had
happened, his eyes glued to the kneeling stool. I wanted to tell him
he wasn't the one who should feel ashamed, who should hide. I
didn't say a word though, and crossed myself when he whispered to
me, "Give thanks to the Lord."

The smell of incense overwhelmed me and the gold and bronze
Jesus over the altar kept staring at me, but I stared back, asking:
How could you let this happen? The priest spoke of the resurrection of
the body and the salvation of the soul, and I thought of my mother
stripping naked and letting Mr. Colombo hold her and kiss her, his
rough lips tickling her bosom. I thought of Maddalena, of how I
wished I could just run to her and tell her everything. I thought of
Tiziano and the creepy smile he'd aimed at me outside the church.

The congregation stood and began queueing to receive the Holy
Communion, the windows shaking as the organ blasted out *"Panis
Angelicus."* I took refuge in the little chapel, where I could be alone
and light a candle: maybe, if I prayed to his mother, the Lord would
listen to what I had to say.

The statue of the Virgin Mary was light blue and gold, a crown
of stars on her head. Someone had wrapped rosary beads around
her wrists and she seemed to look at me kindly, her welcoming arms
held open. Surrounded by the warm scent of wax, I kneeled and
closed my eyes, clasping my hands together. I prayed for Maddalena
and for Luigia, who would never dance with Ernesto again. Then I
thought of the Colombos, of Tiziano who'd almost killed Donatella,
of his father, who, like him, used women as and when he fancied, taking his pleasure as if it was owed to him. I didn't know if one could

ask the Virgin Mary to send someone to hell—but she was a woman too. Surely she would understand.

I took a deep breath, and that's when I caught the nauseating stench of cologne, heard the wooden bench creak, felt hot breath on the back of my neck. "Don't worry, it's me."

Startled, I opened my eyes. Tiziano was kneeling next to me. I tried to stand, but he began stroking me. "Don't tell me you're afraid?" he teased, his voice mellow.

I couldn't speak. His cold fingers caressed the inside of my elbow all the way down to my wrist, slowly, gently, then his hand stole to my hip. "I won't hurt you," he said, like a prayer, then lifted my skirt just enough to slide his hand underneath. I couldn't move, couldn't think. There was nothing but his cold skin on mine and silk brushing up my now-bare thighs. The Virgin Mary looked on. Tiziano's fingers pressed hard between my legs then moved in circles, sending an unexpected hot wave of pain and pleasure crashing over my body. I gripped the pew.

Tiziano moaned, his mouth at my ear. "Sshh," he whispered while his fingers dipped below the waistband of my panties. I was a melted candle, putty in his hands. I wanted to scream, kick, but fear and revulsion had banished my conscience to a place I couldn't reach.

Suddenly he peeled away from me and stood, barely a trace of color on his cheeks. I was still kneeling, nails sinking in the wooden pew, bathed in self-loathing. His mellow whisper again: "I'll be seeing you."

26.

*I*t was Noè who found me, tears marring my face, legs covered in scratches in my haste to slide down the collapsed section of the embankment. I didn't even realize that's what I was doing, as if my body, searching for a safe place to hide, had chosen for me. "Francesca!" he shouted down from the bridge. I looked up and he dropped his bike, rushing to me.

"What happened?" he asked, crouching down next to me.

"Go away!" I yelled, sobbing.

I felt dirty, wrong. I didn't want him to touch me. I only wanted him to let me disappear.

He hesitated, as if I might break, then his hand came to rest on my shoulder, and he called my name. I pushed him away, enraged, screeching like a goose when you grab it by the neck. He froze, hands held up, breathing through his mouth and looking at me with desperate eyes. "What did they do to you?"

What happened afterward I found out the following Sunday, from the old ladies whispering outside the church.

The greengrocer's son had gone to the café at the corner of Piazza dell'Arengario and told Tiziano Colombo, who sat with his friends next to the pastry display case, drinking his hot chocolate, that he was "a Fascist bastard who should get on his knees and beg for forgiveness from all the girls he'd dared put his hands on." Nobody had figured out what girls he was referring to, since he hadn't named any names. Tiziano had laughed and told him to get lost, but Noè had grabbed him by the collar and forced him to stand. "I'll smash you into a pulp," he'd said. Or, "I'll punch your nose straight through your skull"—on this detail the old ladies could not reach a consensus.

Noè had thrown the first punch, after Tiziano replied that the girls he was talking about were "just whores." The other customers—men daintily sipping coffee, ladies in felt hats dragging away children with faces smeared in icing sugar—had quietly but promptly made for the door.

As a young man, Tiziano's father had been running with the *Famigerata* boys, one of the most infamous black-shirt militias of the 1920s, clobbering and forcing castor oil down dissidents' throats for the glory of the motherland—and for Tiziano, too, violence was rooted in a strong sense of justice: smashing heads was a form of liturgy.

The old ladies outside the church said Tiziano's friends had pounced on Tresoldi's son all at once, that Noè had knocked one down—costing him a tooth to boot—and elbowed another in the face, but then someone had landed a kick in his stomach and he'd fallen on his back on one of the tables, sending the hand-painted teacups and silver cutlery flying. Once down, he didn't stand a chance. They'd punched and kicked him—stomach, back, groin. Before they walked away, leaving him for dead, blood and saliva oozing from his nose and mouth, his breath a wheeze, Tiziano had planted a foot in his face, saying, "Vermin."

Colombo had interceded on their behalf with the town and district council, and as a result nobody was punished. People simply stopped asking questions. Even Tresoldi, who couldn't risk losing the shop he'd got through those very same people, had to keep quiet, aside from the cursing, which could be heard two streets away.

When I went to see Noè, his father turned me away, saying that it was just not done and it was all my fault. God knows he'd given his son his fair share of beatings, but the agonized look on his face told me that, this time, he'd been the first to fear for Noè's life.

"Please," I begged. "I just want to see him. Tell him I'm sorry. That he shouldn't have done that."

"All I know about this sorry business is that it ended with my son beaten to a pulp!" Tresoldi yelled, but his voice didn't frighten me anymore. Now I knew mellow voices were the truly dangerous ones. "People were right all along," Tresoldi continued. "You and the Cursed One are bad news."

With nowhere to go and nowhere to hide, I ran to Maddalena's. I arrived at Via Marsala just before dinnertime, my sides aching from exertion, face wet with tears. "It's me," I said through the door. No answer. "Please," I pressed on. "I need you."

Maddalena opened the door without a word. She was wearing an old ratty blouse and a pleated skirt, and looked so changed in those months, as if she'd grown all of a sudden and nothing she wore fit her anymore. She was clutching a letter, so crumpled I imagined she must have read it and read it until her eyes bled. A fierce wave of affection washed over me, and I realized how intensely painful being without her had been, now that she stood there, whole, in front of me, saying, "Come on in."

Mrs. Merlini was making risotto in the kitchen and the pungent smell of saffron filled the room. Donatella, dress stretched across her swollen belly, was setting plates on the table. Her face was dull, no powder, no lipstick. She looked at me with vacant eyes, then turned the other way.

Maddalena led me to her bedroom. "Tell me."

And I told her everything. Words gushed out of me like water from a cracked dam, faster, harder, crumbling all barriers. I told her about my shame and disgust when Tiziano had touched me in church, about Noè, who'd found me crying under Leoni bridge, and later, because of me, had ended up a pile of broken bones.

She listened to me in silence, gritting her teeth. When she looked up, her gaze was sure and firm—the eyes of someone who'd made a decision from which there was no turning back. She handed me the letter she'd been clutching—it was from Ernesto. He must have written it a few days before his condition had worsened: it was dated January 22, but the post office stamp was from the beginning of March. Ernesto had been dead two months, and then Maddalena received a letter from him. It must have felt like a message from the afterworld.

"I'm better," the letter read. "They take good care of me and I'm not skipping a single meal. I promise I'll be back soon, because I have no intention of leaving you, Donatella, and Luigia. You are the most precious things in my life. But if God were to call me to his side, then it'll have to be you looking after them. I'm proud of you. You're a strong girl. Never let anyone dim your faith. I'll keep you in my prayers. Ernesto."

Maddalena laced her fingers through mine as I finished reading. "I'm sorry I wasn't there for you. I just wanted to die. But now I know what I have to do. If you want, we can do it together."

27.

I'm done being good," said Maddalena that mid-March morning. A murky sun appeared in the sky, still shrouded in the
dregs of the night, as we made our way to the Lambro to face
Tiziano. Maddalena had told me we'd find him there waiting for us.
Alone. All it took was a letter delivered to one of the waiters at Caffè
dell'Arengario, with precise instructions for it to land in the right
hands—a fifty-lira note had sealed the deal. She hadn't told me what
she'd written in that letter, only that she'd signed it as Donatella.

"He'll be there," she reassured me as we walked briskly side by
side down Via Vittorio Emanuele, past the bakery and the haberdasher's, their shutters still down. The streets were so empty and
indifferent, they reminded me of a graveyard.

"And what are we going to do then?"

Maddalena didn't answer, stuffing a hand in the pocket of her un-
buttoned coat. She only wore a light dress underneath, and her legs
were purple from the cold. She pulled out Luigia's tailor's shears,
the blades glinting in the dim light.

My breath hitched. "What do you plan on doing with those?"

"You'll see."

I remembered Noè's geese, and his words: "You have to grab the
neck like this, so they'll open their beak."

"You can't."

"Yes, I can."

"And what happens afterward?"

"I don't care," she ground out, shears and hand disappearing back into her pocket.

Leoni bridge was down there, looking much the same and yet bigger, imposing almost, suspended in silence and anticipation under the still-lit streetlamps. The whole place was holding its breath.

We couldn't see him when we leaned over the parapet, but we heard him singing. We climbed down the collapsed section of the embankment, Maddalena holding my hand when we landed so my smooth soles wouldn't slip on the pebbles. Tiziano was there, underneath the arches, in his perfectly pressed uniform pants and clean shirt, Fascist Party pin glinting on his coat. He looked so wrong in that place I associated with happy memories, surrounded by the familiar smell of the river, that I felt as if I'd been slapped in the face. He was singing *"Parlami d'amore Mariù"* under his breath as he skipped stones on the gray water.

Maddalena's palm was clammy despite the cold, her breath labored, mouth wide open. She let go of my hand and stepped toward him. "Over here!"

Tiziano spun around looking confused, then he spotted us and a strange expression spread across his face. "What are you doing here?" he said, discarding the stones he still held in his hand.

"It was me. I wrote the letter," replied the Cursed One. "You have to apologize for the things you did."

"I don't have to apologize for anything. Anything at all."

"You make me sick," Maddalena spat out. "You're a coward who is too afraid to go to war!"

I wanted to say something as well, or at least step closer to her, but as soon as I looked at Tiziano I felt his fingers and his breath on me again, and I couldn't move.

"You know nothing. You're just little girls." He shrugged, stroked his pin, then continued: "You have no idea what my father would have done to me if he'd found out. How could I tell him I was having a baby with a girl like her? You have just . . . no idea." He shook his head hard and his face clouded, chasing thoughts we couldn't see. "And then again, was it actually her—your sister, I mean?" he continued, running his tongue across his teeth. "All cats are gray at night. They all moan and scream the same, you know? You can never be sure once the lights go off . . ."

"You convinced her to be with you," Maddalena pressed him, "because otherwise you wouldn't marry her. Then when her bleeding stopped you pretended to forget and left her, and told everyone in town she was a whore!"

Her determination scared me.

Tiziano licked his lips. "All women should be like the duce's women, who know how to give without asking anything in return. And she wanted that baby, wanted it at all costs. But I can't, you see? I can't. The choice was made for me."

"We'll tell everyone what you did to Donatella and Francesca!" Maddalena shouted.

He burst out laughing, that full, throaty laughter of his. "You're nothing. Who will believe you?" He stepped closer, defiant. "Whatever happens, they'll believe *me*," he added.

"Let's go," I whispered to Maddalena. "Please, let's go away."

But she didn't budge, looking at Tiziano with fierce contempt.

"You're going to die now," she said, in the same voice she'd used with Filippo and Matteo in Tresoldi's backyard. "You're afraid now, you feel you're going to get hurt. Something bad'll happen to you.

Maybe you won't be able to breathe anymore, maybe the rats will eat your eyes."

I stood still, waiting, while Tiziano laughed and kept moving toward us. Something was bound to happen. He was close, so close now that my nose caught a whiff of his cologne, the one I remembered from church.

"What was that, huh?" Tiziano asked. "You trying to scare me, Cursed One?" He wasn't laughing anymore.

Maddalena sought my eyes, fear and rage flashing in hers. Tiziano was right in front of her now, grabbing her by the lapels of her coat.

"And you think I'm scared of two little girls?"

"Yes," Maddalena answered as she hit him on the ear, hard. Tiziano let out an agonizing cry and shook her, his other hand flying to his bleeding temple. She thrashed and squirmed out of her coat, sending Tiziano flying backward on the pebbles, clutching at the empty fabric.

Maddalena still gripped the shining shears, now stained red. Incredulous, Tiziano looked at the blood on his hand. "You think you can kill me, you fucking whores?" he yelled.

Maddalena pounced on him wielding the shears, but Tiziano grabbed her wrist and twisted her arm behind her back. It was her scream that shook me out of my stupor and fear. "Let go of her!" I shouted, lunging at them.

Pain came first: a smack on my jaw, so hard my teeth clamped on my tongue. Then blood came spurting out of my mouth and I slumped to the ground, convinced I was about to die, fighting for air while Tiziano massaged his knuckles. Lying there, icy pebbles under my neck and back, I found myself observing the scene, numb and detached.

Tiziano bent over Maddalena and grabbed a fistful of her hair, twisting it around his fingers and shaking her hard. Her eyes were swollen, blood streaming down her face. She wailed, scratching at his hands to free herself from his grip. She was kicking and screaming mean words, vulgar insults I'd never heard her use before. Tiziano kicked away the shears, which ended up in the Lambro together with a handful of pebbles. Then he dragged Maddalena into the river. One hand on her back, the other still gripping her hair, he pushed her under the water. Maddalena's cry faded into a terrified gurgle.

I couldn't even scream.

Tiziano sang, still keeping her head under the water, the lyrics interspersed with frantic breaths. *"Parlami d'amore, Mariù . . ."* His voice had lost all traces of politeness. It was manic, tainted by a note of perverse satisfaction. Then he waded out of the river, his pants and coat soaked, golden hair glued to his wet forehead. Behind him, Maddalena was on her hands and knees in the water, coughing her lungs out, face covered in blood and mud.

I tried to push myself up on my elbows but kept slipping on the slimy pebbles. Tiziano looked at me and smiled, tongue skating across his teeth. "Now you'll get what's coming to you."

I felt the fear of being alone with a man, at his mercy. It was different from the fear I'd always felt around Tresoldi—that was a lump in your belly, same as when they told us scary stories about ogres and witches. This fear, fear of Tiziano, was all over my body, thick and black, penetrating every fiber.

"Try it and I'll kill you," I said.

Maybe that's what it meant to be a grown-up, to be a woman: not bleeding once a month, not compliments or nice clothes. It was staring at a man who says, *"You belong to me,"* and answering, *"I don't belong to anybody."*

What happened next, I couldn't explain. It was like the things you see in a dream.

Tiziano began frantically rummaging under my skirt. He grabbed my panties and yanked them down to my ankles, then thrust his knees in between my thighs, forcing my legs open. I screamed, pummeled his back and shoulders, but he had me pinned to the ground. Then he gripped my wrists and locked my arms above my head, saying, "Hush now, be still."

I loathed him, loathed myself, loathed everything. His breathing was labored, face white, lips purple, as if his soul had been sucked out of him.

"I can hear the devil coming," a voice came from the river, hoarse and feral. I turned and saw Maddalena crawling out of the Lambro, rivulets of water dripping on the stones, blood running down her forehead. "Says he'll rip your heart out himself."

Tiziano laughed, prized my lips open, pushed his tongue in.

"He'll rip it out with his teeth! And he'll drag you down to hell!" Maddalena continued.

Tiziano pushed himself up and stuck a hand down his pants to find that hard, throbbing thing that strained against the fabric. Then, suddenly, as if someone had flicked a switch, he froze, his eyes two black pits brimming with fear—the eyes of a child.

He sagged on top of me, breathing on my neck for a few more seconds: scorching, violent bursts of air. And then he wasn't moving anymore.

The Shape of a Voice

*W*as it his sick heart that did him in, or did the Cursed One stop him with her voice?

I walked home, feet soaked, skin like ice, the taste of blood lingering in my mouth, and I kept wondering. I could see his face, twisted in a grimace, I could feel his hands holding me down. I ached all over, even my teeth ached, my bones. And yet, for all the fear and loathing, my thoughts were of Maddalena, of her hand clasping mine as she said she'd see me soon.

The following day came, unbidden. As the hours slid mindlessly into one another, I could only think of that body lying in the river. I was terrified we'd be found out and prayed that everything around us would just disappear, leaving only Maddalena and me. But prayers can't keep the world at bay, and by the time the Cursed One came to find me—"We have to tell Noè. He can help us hide the body"—the search parties had already been sent out. Tiziano Colombo's corpse was discovered one morning, under a sky so heavy it looked like lumps of sodden wool.

They said it had been Filippo, his brother, who suggested looking near the Lambro. He knew Tiziano was headed there to meet someone—someone who'd set a trap for him, perhaps. A dissident in all likelihood, who wanted to destabilize one of the town's most esteemed families in order to strike a blow against the Fascist regime, which the Colombos had always staunchly supported.

The rats had gnawed out his eyes and tongue, and the rest of the body was caked in mud, nostrils and ears completely clogged, so much so that even Mrs. Colombo had trouble identifying her son. She clasped his pin in her fist and said, "Justice will be done. This despicable crime shall not go unpunished"—or that's what the local paper printed, anyway.

Mr. Colombo declared himself pleased with the front-page article, for which he'd personally selected a portrait of his son, wearing his Fascist uniform and Hollywood smile. He was disappointed, however, when the national papers devoted a scant column to the tragedy, without even naming the victim.

Two days later, toward the end of March, they found the letter from Donatella. Colombo's eldest son hadn't been killed by a Communist after all. Not a dissident either, nor a traitor or an anarchist, which would have made Tiziano nothing short of a martyr. No, it had been a girl, cheap as they come, a "swallow," without a father, her belly swelling with a bastard. When the secret police turned up at her door at dawn, she was in her nightgown, barefoot. They took her in like that, not even letting her grab a shawl. Her mother's and sister's cries woke the whole building.

That same evening, my mother came to see me. "I bought train tickets for Naples. We leave tomorrow, you and I. We'll be staying with my family for a while."

"Why?" I asked, breath hitching in my throat.

She wouldn't answer.

It was my father who explained what had happened. The Fascists had hauled Donatella to the police station to interrogate her:

"Why won't you do the Fascist salute?"

"I didn't know I had to . . ."

"Did you know the victim?"

"Yes, yes, of course I knew him, he was my boyfriend."

"What happened?"

"I told him about the baby and he didn't want to see me anymore."

"Whose baby?"

"His! The baby is his, who else's?"

"The victim's family assured us their son would never engage in fornication outside of marriage—the baby must be someone else's, someone who paid you for your services and wasn't careful enough, perhaps?"

"No . . . never! That's not true!"

"What about this letter, then?"

"I've never seen this letter!"

"That's your name on it—how do you explain that?"

"I didn't write it! I swear to God, I swear!"

Who would believe that disheveled girl, belly swelling with a baby that hadn't been put there by her husband? A woman of ill repute who wouldn't know truth if it hit her in the face?

My father also told me that the youngest Merlini daughter had been shouting unspeakable insults against the deceased: that he treated women like animals, used them then threw them away, and groped little girls in church. It was then that my name had come up and my mother decided we had to leave. She hadn't asked me anything, hadn't even looked at me, as if she was ashamed of me. She'd started packing, carelessly throwing clothes and curling irons into her suitcase. While she was yelling at Carla to find her polka dot summer dress and sandals, my father came to me.

I was sitting in the kitchen, a slice of vanilla cake Carla had baked especially for me still untouched on the table. I hadn't eaten in days. A relentless nausea wrenched my stomach and climbed all the way up the back of my neck, clogging my brain.

Dad was silent for a long spell, rubbing his thumb over his knuckles, then he cleared his throat. "What they're saying . . ." he began, running his tongue across his lips. He swallowed. "I mean . . . what they're saying happened in church . . . in the Virgin Mary chapel . . . what he . . . did to you . . ." He hesitated again, took a breath. "I'm sorry that happened, I am so very sorry. It's not your fault, you know that?"

I gave a small, barely perceptible nod.

"You didn't do anything wrong, you know that, right?"

"I don't want to go with Mom."

"I know. I know, Francesca."

"Why are you sending me away?"

"I don't want you to go. I really don't. But maybe it's for the best, you know? Just for a little while, I promise, until things sort themselves out."

His fingers grazed my shoulder, as if he was afraid to touch me. I sagged against him and hugged him, burying my face in his chest. He jerked, then something seemed to loosen inside him and he wrapped his arms around me, his chin digging into the crook of my neck as he stroked my hair. He smelled like his shirts in the wardrobe, the ones I hid my face in when I needed to scream.

It was still dark when we arrived at the train station. My mother hobbled along, clasping her too-heavy suitcase. Hat all askew, a beaten look on her face, she shouldered through the crowd. "Excuse us," she whimpered in a shy, tired voice, the undone ribbon on her collar dangling down her front, silk stockings laddered all the way from the back of her knee to her heel.

White steam from the train wheels rose to the cast-iron rafters, pushing its way into my nose, scorching it. "Move," my mother said, grabbing my elbow and jerking me forward. "Behave!"

I thought about Donatella, who would swell like a toad, all alone, and end up hating the baby growing inside her, curled up in the dark. I thought about Mrs. Merlini, who—if the Lord had spared her sons and protected her daughter—might just have found some room in her heart for Maddalena. As it was, however, she'd be burying herself deeper and deeper in grief. I thought of the apartment on Via Marsala, of the copper pots casting long shadows across that kitchen, which grew emptier by the day.

And I thought about Maddalena. About her voice when she'd told Tiziano the devil would rip his heart out, about her hand clasping mine, about the smell of the river.

Pain was a thing you could touch: stomach in knots, swollen bladder, blood thumping against my skull. I was a broken bone.

I knew I'd never see her again. I was abandoning her. I was there too, that day by the river when Tiziano had died. Maddalena defended me, she saved me like the hero in a novel. Once again, someone else would shoulder the blame for the things I'd done. I let my mother drag me to the platform where the engine was already waiting, decorated with a brass wheat sheaf emblem. People smelled of broken sleep and the first cigarettes of the day. My mind was blank, legs shaky.

That's when I heard someone call out to me: "Francesca! Wait!" Noè was on his toes, clinging to one of the columns under the train timetables, straining to be seen over the crowd.

I froze. My mother almost tripped when she tried to yank me forward, but I slipped out of her grip and ran to him.

"What are you doing here?"

"You have to come with me," he said in a rush of breath. "Right now." His nose was crooked and covered in scabs. Yellow bruises ringed his eyes, a deep, stitched wound ran the length of his brow.

"I can't."

"Yes, you can."

I couldn't look him in the eye. It was as if I was made of glass.

"I can't," I repeated.

"Are you scared?"

"Of course I'm scared. Tiziano is dead!"

"I know. Maddalena confessed. She said she killed him."

"But that's not true!" I blurted out. "It was his sick heart—he just dropped dead!" Or maybe it had been Maddalena's voice that stopped his heart, maybe she'd really killed him.

"It doesn't matter anymore."

I felt like newspaper crumpling in the fire. "What's going to happen to her?"

Noè shook his head, enraged, then had to stop because of the pain. "I don't know. She tried to tell the truth about that bastard, but they didn't believe her. It's the Cursed One's word against the word of a Fascist."

"And what can *I* do?"

Noè's eyes narrowed into hostile slits. "You can tell the truth too."

"And why would they believe *me*?"

"Don't you even want to try?" Iodine tincture and ointment blotted out Noè's familiar smell, that earthy scent I so liked.

"I don't know that I can do it. I'm not like her. My words count for nothing." I hid my face in shame and self-loathing as the train whistled, my mother calling out to me.

"It's my IOU," Noè said.

"Your IOU?"

"For the clementines. You owe me."

"I can't do it."

"Francesca, we have to go!" my mother shouted behind my back.

"Not even for her?"

I forced myself to look at him, to seek his eyes in that wrecked face. Wrecked because of me.

"I'm not like you and I'm not like her," I said "I can't. I can't do it!"

"Don't make me say it again, Missy. Get on the train, now!"

A porter had helped my mother haul her suitcase onto the carriage and she was gesturing at me to join her, arms flailing out of the window, hands encased in white gloves.

"I have to go . . ." I told Noè.

He stared at me without saying a word, and I wondered what would happen to Maddalena now that she had confessed. I had no idea what they would do to her. All I knew about executions came from novels: she'd be decapitated perhaps, or hanged. Or maybe they'd throw her in jail, where she'd be beaten with sticks by nuns in some convent in the country.

My mother was leaning out of the carriage, holding her hand out to me. "Watch the step or you'll ruin your dress."

That's when I froze. Unprompted, my posture and attitude morphed into the Cursed One's. My mind and body were brimming with her, and she came crashing over me when I said, "I don't care about the dress."

I turned and looked for Noè, but he was gone. I ran back up the platform, the crowd parting like cockroaches to let me through. The train was pulling out now, my mother was screaming. I found him outside the station as he retrieved his bike, abandoned against a lamppost. And suddenly I could breathe again, the lump in my chest melting like butter in a frying pan.

"Noè, wait!"

"Utterly ridiculous"—those were Mr. Colombo's words when I requested to speak. The crowd began barking like a pack of hunting dogs who'd spotted a hare, trying to keep me away from Maddalena. She was standing, alone, in the middle of that room with white marble floors and frescoed ceilings, where a blond angel holding the coat of arms of Italy's royal family observed the commotion, indifferent.

She'd been dragged before the mayor, Noè had told me—someone had grabbed her beneath the arms, someone else by the ankles, like a witch carried to the stake, as if the laws of man counted for nothing. The mayor had watched the mob pile into his office, where a tricolor flag and wheat sheaf emblem stood in pride of place, and said, in a miffed tone: "This is not a court of law and I cannot put a child on trial! That's not how it works." And then he and his uniformed officers had laughed at those who thought a dirty, scrawny little girl could kill a grown man. A Fascist, to boot.

"This is no little girl," Mrs. Colombo had shot back, her face a mask of anguish. "This is the Cursed One!"

"Let me through!" I shouted, straining on my toes to seek Maddalena's eyes above the sea of heads. I was still panting, my hair in a tangle from rushing there on Noè's bike, his feet pumping on the pedals. Then I'd run up the town hall staircase and through interminable cavernous corridors, my steps amplified in a chilling echo.

"I have something to say too!"

"And why should we listen to a little girl? What is she doing here? Someone get her father!"

I elbowed my way through the throngs of carabinieri, men wearing their hats indoors, and women clutching their bags. I had to get to the Cursed One, and their screams and threats didn't scare me. Noè tried to stay by my side, but the crowd pushed him back.

Finally, Maddalena looked at me. Her lips moved: "You're back."

"She didn't do it!" It wasn't until the words were out that I realized I'd shouted them.

A row of uniforms, among them Mr. Colombo, stood before us, looking like they'd have gladly crushed us under their boots. Maddalena, however, stared everyone down with bright, brazen eyes, and they, too, ended up believing she could kill with a word. Even those men, who could send you to your death with a flick of their finger, were floored by the Cursed One's gaze. The mayor, medals glinting on his chest, black tassel dangling on his forehead, slammed his fists on the table, demanding silence, but the mob kept howling:

"It's the devil made her do it."

"She's the Cursed One."

"Such a young man—so handsome, so polite."

"Destined for great things."

"And she tossed him in the water like a dead dog."

In their world, there were only two certainties. The first: things that couldn't be explained were the work of the Lord or the devil, depending on whether they befell "ruffians" or "respectable people." The second: men were never to blame.

"You're right!" I said, breathless, standing next to Maddalena. "It was her."

The room went quiet and still as a catacomb.

"And it was me too. And Donatella and the baby growing inside her. It was the Lord and it was the devil. It was the river, and the stones on the riverbank, and his blasted heart. It was all these things that killed him."

The crowd was about to explode.

"Silence!" ordered the mayor.

"You say it never happened because you don't believe a man like him could do those filthy things to girls like us. But that's exactly what he did. And we can't keep quiet anymore."

Maddalena was so beautiful she shone, even on her knees, with smudges of dirt on her face. She rose to her feet and grabbed my hand, her palm warm and clammy. She smiled. I'd never felt so strong in my life.

ACKNOWLEDGMENTS

S aying "thank you" is one of the first things I was taught as a child, I'd say around the same time I learned how to cross the street and began unpicking the mystery that are shoelaces. When you're little, however, you have to say "thank you" even when you don't feel like saying it at all.

Now that I'm a grown-up, I can thank who I want, and for the things that really matter.

Thank you to those who believed in my story enough to give it a chance to be read:

Carmen Prestia, the first to take a chance on me, the first to tell me: "Francesca will forever live in my heart."

Rosella Postorino, for the rigor and meticulous care you brought to my work. Thank you for insisting I add *that* dialogue. And thank you for your stories, which stayed with me.

Roberta Pellegrini, for the precious advice and attention to detail.

Maria Luisa Putti, for staying up until 4 a.m. looking after my story. You worked your magic and made this book the best possible version of itself. Thank you for your obsession with words, and for introducing me to Pessoa.

Paolo Repetti—without you, this book wouldn't exist. Thank you.

Thank you to the Holden creative writing school and its wonderful teachers:

Eleonora Sottili for all the times you told me, "This scene works!" and above all for the times you told me, "This one, however, doesn't work at all."

Federica Manzon for believing in me and for our "doubt-buster" chats in the second-floor office.

Marco Missiroli, because one of the key scenes in this story was conceived in the school gardens, during your mind-blowing lesson.

Andrea Tarabbia for introducing me to Fenoglio's short story *Il Gorgo* ("The Whirlpool"), for the trip to Giardino di Ninfa, and for the grapefruit.

Thank you to Livio Gambarini and Masa Facchini, my irreplaceable mentors on the "pleasures of writing" course at the Università Cattolica, for reading my first, unbearably awkward short stories, and for teaching me to despise scenes that begin with "the light filtering through the curtains." Thank you to Martina, who also read the aforementioned short stories, and kept believing in me nonetheless.

Thank you to Franco Pezzini, Turin's own Van Helsing, for letting me join his wonderful course.

Thank you to Chiara Riboldi, Caterina Muttarini, Enrica Jalongo, Rossana and Laura Portinari, and Massimiliano Tibaldi for being the Virgil to my Dante, safely guiding me out of the inferno that was secondary school.

Thank you to my fellow writers and adventurers: Francesco, indomitable builder of worlds; Alice, who shines like a firefly; Giada, daughter of the moon; Sergio, cynical samurai with a heart of gold; Antonia, sarcastic witch and trusted adviser on all matters of fictional relationships. I couldn't have wished for better company, on a flying ship as on this earth.

Thank you, in no particular order, to the other colleagues from Scrivere B College (class of 2019–2021): Big Vittoria, Little Vittoria, Paola, Simone, Rossella, Giorgia, Lea, Tommaso, Silvia, Mary,

Susanna, Benedetta, Davide, Giovanni, Edo. Thank you for being my first readers and for letting me read your stories. It was like looking into each other's souls. You shine so bright.

Thank you to my friends, because with you, I never feel bad for being myself: Nico, Monza's own Rasputin; Ricky, unbreakable rock; Mario, half-ogre half-master brewer; Jacopo, mountain eagle; and Gabriele, aka Cheshire Cyborg.

Gaia—thank you because throughout those terrible, turbulent school years, the stories we wrote together and the beautiful, crazy characters we dreamed up were often the only flashes of happiness I could find. I carry them in my heart. Thank you for the serving platters, the light fittings, and the nights we stayed up chatting and drinking Sangue di Giuda until dawn.

Beatrice, thank you for always letting me drag you into my mad schemes. Thank you for the interminable study sessions, for our teenage obsessions, and for the horrendous portrait you drew of me, where I look more like a platypus than a human being. Thank you for always being there.

Thank you to my family, my aunts and uncles and cousins who always believed in me, especially Federico, Lorenzo, Marco, and Giulia. I love you.

Mom and Dad, thank you for always supporting this little girl, who, aged nine, ran away from home in search of adventures armed with a blueberry juice box and a book on Aztec civilization tucked into her backpack. The little girl who, when she grew up, wanted to be a knight. If this book is here today, it is thanks to all your "Once upon a times," to my forever-fraying, endlessly mended pockets housing my collection of oddly shaped pebbles, and to all the stars you pointed at, saying, "I wonder who lives up there."

A NOTE FROM THE TRANSLATOR

*I*t is often the case that the title of a book is the very last thing to be translated, and *The Cursed Friend* was no exception. There were so many layers to the Italian original— *La Malnata* translates roughly as someone who was "born wrong," but is commonly used in 1930s Monza, where the story is set, to refer to misbehaving children—so akin to the English "rascal."

With Maddalena, however, there is definitely a more sinister dimension to the nickname. We learn early on in the novel that even adults are afraid of her, or suspicious of her at the very least, due to the rumors circulating about the bad things happening around her. She's not simply a wild child, she's a "witch" who was "kissed by the devil" (as also evidenced by the mark on her face).

To add to the complexity, the nickname (and therefore the title) recurs on almost every page throughout the novel, as this is how Maddalena is most commonly referred to. Last but not least, Maddalena's gang is also referred to as "i Malnati" ("the rascals/bad seeds") on several occasions.

So, in principle, not only did the title have to function in isolation on the cover, as titles do, but it also had to convey the local dialect meaning of "rascal"; serve as Maddalena's nickname with all the added darker connotations of "jinx" and "witch"; and, finally, work in the plural too, so it could be applied to her gang as well.

In the end, something had to give, and a collective decision was made to focus on conveying the prejudice and superstition Maddalena faced, so we (myself, the author, and the editorial team) settled on "cursed." And while "The Cursed One/s" was used throughout, for the title itself we chose "The Cursed Friend," since the story is told from Francesca's point of view.

Something lost, something added—it's the beauty of translation.

Here ends Beatrice Salvioni's
The Cursed Friend.

The first edition of this book was printed
and bound at Lakeside Book Company in
Harrisonburg, Virginia, April 2024.

A NOTE ON THE TYPE

The text of this novel was set in Italian Old Style, a Venetian typeface designed by Frederic W. Goudy in 1924. Initially requested by Monotype to imitate a type by a competitor, Goudy instead convinced the foundry to produce a new typeface. Inspired by fifteenth century Venetian types, Italian Old Style is a reverent and handsome rendition of the Renaissance style.

HARPERVIA

An imprint dedicated to publishing international voices, offering readers a chance to encounter other lives and other points of view via the language of the imagination.